Kaleidoscope of Tales

Humor, Romance, Drama

All of the Above

Kaleidoscope of Tales

Humor, Romance, Drama

All of the Above

a collection of stories by

Mickey Jordan

Kaleidoscope of Tales:
Humor, Romance, Drama, All of the Above

Copyright © 2014 by Mickey Jordan

ISBN-10: 0991355032
ISBN-13: 978-0-9913550-3-7

Freeze Time Media

Cover illustration by John Freeze

This book is dedicated to
Becky
my best friend and loving wife
As long as I have eyes
you'll be admired
As long as I have legs
you'll never walk alone
As long as I have arms
you'll be held
As long as I can breathe
you'll be loved

Acknowledgments

Many writers have provided me with guidance and advice — none more than the members of the Village Writers' Critique Group. They consist of:

John Achor, Linda Black, Jerry Davis, Nancy Foris, Nancy Holder, Janet Holt, Marlene Kloask, Betty Marlow and Mary Lou Moran. Thank you one and all.

Three very special people were actively involved: Becky Jordan, computer transcriber; my adopted mentor, Madelyn Young; and Di Freeze, the editor and publisher. Could not have done it without these three ladies.

Contents

Willie's Dream

My secretary informed me my son was on line one. Since it is unusual for him to call me at my office, I figured it was important.

"Hi, Patrick. What can I do for you?"

"Dad, one of my friends here in Memphis is on the board of directors of Dream Factory. This is an organization similar to Make-A-Wish. They work with young people who are either critically or terminally ill, and arrange for the child to experience his/her fondest desire.

"There is a ten-year-old youngster here in Memphis who is not expected to live. He idolizes Brett Favre, and Dream Factory would like to arrange for him to meet Brett. I told them you knew Brett and played golf with him in the off-season. They asked if you would find out if Brett would be able to meet Willie."

"I can't promise anything. It's football season now, and I'm sure time is of the essence due to Willie's sickness. It may not be possible."

Two days later I telephoned Irvin Favre, Brett's father. I explained the situation to him and asked if he would run it by Brett this weekend when he was attending the game in Green Bay. The following Tuesday Irvin called me. "Brett would be happy to do it," he said, "but we must deal with the Packer organization. We should call Ed Martin at the Green Bay Packers' office to arrange a meeting."

I passed this information on to Dream Factory. Within a month Patrick called me all excited. "It's unbelievable what they did for Willie. The Green Bay Packers flew Willie and his parents to Green Bay on Friday before the game and set them up in a luxurious hotel suite. Saturday morning, Willie was taken to Lambeau Field to meet Brett. He was given his own custom-made jersey. Brett played catch with him and let Willie accompany him through the entire practice. He told Willie, 'I'll throw a touchdown pass for you tomorrow.'"

That evening Willie ate dinner with the team. Of course, he sat with Brett. He was introduced and received a standing ovation. Willie and his parents had seats in the Packers' corporate sky box on the 50-yard line. To make it even more special, the Packers won the game and Brett threw two touchdown passes.

After the game, Willie was escorted down to the field. Brett greeted him, took off the jersey he had worn in the game, presented it to Willie, and gave him a hug.

Three weeks later, my son Patrick called again. "Dad, Willie died last night. Please inform Brett and thank him again."

Irvin returned the following Monday from having watched the previous day's game. He said, "I gave Brett the news, as you asked. Being a father of two, he took it hard. In fact, he teared up."

Later, Patrick had occasion to meet the child's mother, who thanked him profusely. "Willie was a sad little boy most of his life," she said, "but for the last three weeks of his life, after the trip to meet Brett in Green Bay, he couldn't get the smile off his face."

Author's Note: WILLIE'S DREAM

This story is related as it actually occurred. Celebrities frequently are cited for the mistakes and errors they make. That alone is not fair.

Besides being a charitable, heartwarming story, it is representative of the many charitable actions celebrities perform that are never recognized.

Today Brett is a true family man: husband, father, and grandfather. He recently rejected an offer to return to the NFL.

Willie's Dream won an award from the 2012 Springfield, Missouri Writers Guild in the Prose: Non-Fiction Category. It also was awarded at the Arkansas Writers' Conference 2013. Finally, by invitation, I read it on the Tales of the South radio program from Little Rock, Arkansas. It was broadcast on PBS to more than 20,000 radio shows and podcasts.

Mother's Day Gifts

Mother's Day was only ten days away. Leon would have to work fast if he was going to please both Elizabeth and Ginger.

He recalled Elizabeth's words: "I'd really like a set of non-stick frying pans. I saw some recently at Dillard's. They would match the décor of the kitchen — red."

For twenty-six years, his wife had spent many hours in the kitchen. So, he was happy to oblige her wish.

Ginger was another story. He'd been seeing her for seven weeks. She was a thirty-three-year-old divorcee who worked at his office. Being an attractive, shapely, young lady, she fulfilled his fantasy. Since she was the mother of three, he wanted to get her a present too.

He recalled Ginger's words on the previous Thursday. "Leon, sweetie, you're such an amazing lover. You make me feel so good." Reflecting on that, he bought Ginger's gift at Victoria's Secret. It was a pair of long, black stockings and a black garter belt. He could visualize her curvaceous body in them, and that excited him.

Pleased with his purchases, all he needed was to wrap the gifts and enclose Mother's Day cards to accompany them. With the lingerie, he wrote on the card, "Hope to see you with these on Thursday afternoon." The card that went with the fry pans read, "I know you will do great things with these."

On Saturday, Leon was home alone. Elizabeth had a hair appointment, so he seized the opportunity to wrap both presents, and he enclosed the cards. Then he hid them in the trunk of his car for clandestine safekeeping.

The Friday before Mother's Day he gave Ginger her present in a brown grocery sack, which she could take home with the gift concealed. He cautioned her not to open the box until the morning of Mother's Day.

He also planned to present Elizabeth's gift to her on Mother's Day morning after breakfast. As they sat and enjoyed their final cup of coffee, he handed her the box.

Imagine his shock when Elizabeth unwrapped the sexy black hose and garter belt. She gasped, and he almost fell off his chair. After reading the card, she said, "You know Thursday is my bridge day. Besides, how could you meet me in the afternoon? You work every afternoon. No wonder I could never reach you on Thursday afternoons! You obviously were sneaking off to see another woman."

This rendered him speechless. Obviously, her suspicion was warranted.

Twenty minutes later, Leon answered a call on his cell phone. It was from Ginger and she was obviously irate and stunned. She practically shouted, "Leon, I so looked forward to your gift. It's one thing to receive frying pans and another to be told, 'I know you'll do great things with these.'"

Her voice grew louder, and she shouted, "I thought

we had romance. All you are looking for are home-cooked meals. You can forget our Thursday afternoon meeting and future meetings!" That being said, Leon heard her slam down her phone and the line went dead.

No doubt about it, switching the gifts was the biggest mistake of his life!

Ginger no longer will see Leon. In fact, she doesn't return his telephone calls.

As you can imagine, by just mentioning the events at the beauty parlor, Elizabeth might just as well have erected a billboard. Her phone frequently rings from her lady friends expressing outrage and condolences. Elizabeth reasoned, if we can afford gifts for another woman, I can spend whatever I wish. I'm going to buy the things I've always wanted but avoided for economic reasons. Elizabeth decided to take an extended cruise of the Greek Islands. She is traveling alone with her newly acquired wardrobe from Saks Fifth Avenue.

Virtually the entire community is aware of Leon's blunder. Leon has become almost a hermit. He travels to work each morning. At the end of the day he promptly goes home. He keeps his blinds closed, and, because of his embarrassment, he is seldom seen.

Author's Note: MOTHER'S DAY GIFTS

Wrapping gifts for my family at Christmas time was always a challenge for me. Often, after putting the paper and ribbon (often with bows) on the presents, it was confusing regarding who was to get which gift. On more than one occasion I mixed up the recipients.

It occurred to me how embarrassing it could be outside the family. That led to my visualizing the dilemma that would occur as described in "Mother's Day Gifts."

Backyard Battle

My wife, Betty, and I are bird watchers. Mind you, we could not be classified as card-carrying orni-thologists. Our enjoyment is sitting in our home and watching the graceful creatures as they descend to enjoy the birdseed.

Until six months ago we placed our bird feeder on the side of the house adjacent to the wooded lot next door. We don't have just any bird feeder; we bought the more expensive one, the type whose pole runs from the ground up passing through a dead-end cylinder. The feed is stored on top of the cylinder.

On many occasions we have witnessed squirrels climb the pole only to be frustrated, as they could not get to the feed. The pet store manager advised Betty to place the feeder at least twelve feet from any trees or vines so the pesky squirrels could not leap to the top of the feeder. And so she did. All was fine for several months.

Betty later said, "Let's move the bird feeder to the rear of our house. There it will be more visible and we can observe the birds for a greater period of time."

This proved to be a good move and we enjoyed considerably more viewing of our feathered friends.

We use our kitchen table for many activities. Besides food preparation, eating, and other kitchen chores, it often serves as a desk because of the large surface on which to work. It is in an alcove surrounded in glass. A great viewing area. Everything seemed fine until Betty found the feeder completely emptied on several consecutive mornings. She observed, "This has never happened before."

One evening as she was having a cup of coffee, she spied the culprit. Seated on top of the bird feeder was a large raccoon dumping the birdseed to the ground as he had dinner. Because of his size and climbing expertise, the dead-end cylinder was no obstacle for him.

Having been married to Betty for many years, I've learned not to challenge her. She is tenacious. Thus began the battle of the raccoon versus Betty.

One evening she spotted our raccoon nemesis ambling out of the next-door woods headed for the feeder. She stepped outside by the feeder and the intruder stopped, looked at her, and hissed menacingly. That frightened her, and she turned on the backyard garden hose and sprayed him. He took off running back to the woods to his safety nest.

For four or five days there was no sign of the raccoon. Betty stated, "Let's hope the hose incident discouraged him forever."

Wrong!

One week later he returned. Since Betty could not sit at the kitchen table all the time, she needed another weapon. While visiting at our son's home and telling him of our problem, Betty listened to him talk about a trap he once used to capture several squirrels in his attic. "Hmm. That could be the answer to my dilemma," she mused.

She baited the trap with birdseed and placed it between the wooded lot and the feeder. The first two nights failed. Both mornings, the trap was on its side and the birdseed was gone, with not a critter in sight. My wife surmised, "The coon's size makes the squirrel trap ineffective."

Her final solution worked and is now being used. Each evening as it starts to get dark (the raccoon only invades at night), she places a pillowcase over the cylinder. Betty secures the bottom of it with a rubber band. Each morning she removes the cover, and the birds begin their breakfast.

Betty, a golfer, has made a rare hole-in-one. She has been queen of a Mardi Gras krewe. She has given birth and raised three healthy and successful sons. But, she considers victory over conquering the raccoon to be one of the most gratifying accomplishments in her life.

Author's Note: BACKYARD BATTLE

Backyard Battle occurred over a period of two months. It was a case of perseverance and determination. Both combatants were resolute and stubborn. It was quite a study in the resiliency and cleverness of both. It is still difficult to determine who should be declared the winner.

Collision

It begins as do most football running plays. The guard pulls out, leads the way, and blocks the defensive end. The fullback then follows, runs through the gap that has been created, and seeks the linebacker to engage him. No deception here. The intent is to overpower the defense, not trick them.

That leaves the ball carrier unimpeded. He heads towards me, a defensive halfback. Now it's one on one, man against man.

If he veers towards the sidelines, I could push him out of bounds. However, I've been taught to attempt to influence him to run toward the middle of the field where other defenders might assist me. Of course, he could choose to just run straight ahead in an attempt to barrel me over. Should that occur, I'm confident that all those hours spent in the weight room have prepared me to have the strength to punish him.

Remember what you've been taught. Runners use their heads, arms, and legs to fake a defender of their intent. Focus on the ball carrier's navel. Where it goes, the rest of him goes.

Now the ball carrier is a mere three feet away. I can see his eyes and hear his breathing. The roar of the crowd grows louder as the distance between us narrows. I smell perspiration. It makes no difference if it's his or mine.

Remain relaxed now. It allows for quicker movement. Let your instincts take over. Brace yourself.
COLLISION!

Author's Note: COLLISION

The basis of this story comes from the fact that I played football for eight years. Also, the teaching I received from various coaches during that time influenced me.

Words cannot express how rapidly the detailed action takes place. Further, the quick mental as well as physical adjustments and actions occur very swiftly.

Finally, successfully playing your position brings a satisfaction and pride that is difficult to comprehend.

For all readers who have participated in organized football, you know what I mean.

Demons

"Tournament office! Tournament office! Help!" the walkie-talkie blared.

"This is the tournament office."

"Becky, there's a man down out here. He's lying on the ground on the golf course!" The marshal reported.

"Where are you?"

"Between the third green and the fourth tee."

"I'll be right out. Keep him quiet and wait there so you can help me put him in the golf cart."

What a way to start off Monday of tournament week. This was the first day that we had moved our temporary offices to the Windance Country Club, the tournament site, and the third year that my husband, Mickey, and I were co-tournament directors of the Mississippi Gulf Coast Classic. Experience taught us to expect the unexpected.

I called 911, ordered an ambulance, and hastily drove a golf cart to where the man lay. People nearby said he was a caddy. With some help we placed him in the passenger side of the golf cart, and I drove the caddy back to the clubhouse with me. We laid him on a couch.

He was conscious, although his face was pale and

he was quite weak. I placed wet, cool compresses on his forehead. Then I struck up a conversation to help him relax and learn more about him.

"What's your name?"

He stared up at me with bleary eyes.
"Richard Weaver."

"Where are you from, Richard?"

"Memphis."

I smiled. "That's a long way from the Coast. What are you doing down here?"

"I'm a tour caddy. I work for a golf professional and I travel each week to the locations of the tournament." As we spoke his coloring improved but his moaning revealed he still had much discomfort.

The two Professional Golf Association (PGA) gentlemen, assigned to supervise the players, were quite alarmed. They knew the caddy and said the pro he caddies for hadn't arrived yet. They urged Richard to take the ambulance and go to a hospital for observation.

"I will only go to a hospital if she takes me," he said, gesturing to me.

I called Mickey on his walkie-talkie. "What should I do?"

"Drive him to the hospital. Failure to do so could be interpreted as negligence. Once he's at the hospital, come back promptly. We still have a lot to do."

As we pulled out of the parking lot, I inquired, "Are you feeling better?"

"Yes, ma'am."

"Good, I didn't realize it was so hot today."

"It's probably not that."

I began to sense he might just have a hangover.

"Oh, out having too much fun last night? We've all done that. Do you have a family?"

"Not married. How about you?"

"I have six children and I'm proud of them all."

He responded, "Good."

"I'm going to take you to Singing River Hospital, which is nearby."

"Maybe we should go to Ocean Springs Hospital."

I was surprised to find he knew the area. "I didn't think you were from around here."

He didn't meet my eyes. "I heard Ocean Springs is a good hospital."

There seemed to be more to this story.

A bit later he asked, "Can we stop at that 7-11 for a drink?"

"Sure, but not for a beer," I teased.

When I got back into the car with two sodas, he became more talkative. "I'm a binge drinker. I fell off the wagon this past weekend. I don't drink all the time, but when I do, I can't stop. Since Stewart didn't make the cut last week, I came here early and had too much time on my hands." He began to cry. "I checked myself into Ocean Springs Hospital after drinking for three days straight. I had to dry out."

I was sorry to hear that. I told him, "We have a son, Patrick, who's a recovering alcoholic. He hasn't had a drink in six years. As a matter of fact, he'll be here Thursday. I know hc would talk with you. It's tough to stop."

"No kidding. I don't think I can."

"Sure you can. I'm certain Patrick didn't think he could stop either."

Richard changed the conversation. "Tell me more about your family."

I spent several minutes doing so. I thought about telling him of our fifteen-year- old son who was killed in a car accident three years ago but decided not to bring up this sad fact.

Richard asked, "Do you play golf?"

"Yes."

"So do I. It's an honorable game — players call penalties on themselves!"

We pulled up to the emergency entrance, and Richard gave me a sheepish smile. "How did you know I drink too much?"

"Just a feeling I had. A lucky guess. Let's get you taken care of so you can caddy for your pro."

"Okay."

As we entered the hospital, a nurse walked by us and said to Richard, "We knew you'd be back."

I looked at Richard, puzzled. He said, "I checked myself out."

I helped Richard to a seat and went to the admitting window. "The man with me is in pretty bad shape. Please get to him as soon as possible." She assured me she would, despite having a waiting room of many people.

I walked over to Richard. "Just wait here 'till they call you. I have to get back to work. Here's my business card with my telephone number. If you have any questions or problems, call me. Don't do anything foolish."

"Don't worry, Ms. Becky. I'll be okay."

After returning to my office, I informed everyone about what had happened. Then I returned to my work and got involved in my projects.

About forty-five minutes later, my telephone rang. "Tournament director's office."

"May I speak to Rebecca Jordan?"

"This is she."

"Ms. Jordan, this is Sheriff Joe Walls. Were you in Ocean Springs today with anyone?"

"Yes, I was."

"Would you describe the person you were with?"

"He wore jeans and a short-sleeve yellow shirt and sneakers. I'd say he was in his early thirties. Oh, and he had brown hair."

"I'm not sure how to tell you this, but the man you described jumped off a bridge onto the interstate and committed suicide a little while ago."

"Oh, my God."

"Do you know his name?"

"Richard Weaver."

"The only piece of identification on him was your business card in one of his pants pockets. Ms. Jordan, we need to ask you some questions. Will you be at the country club today?"

"Yes, all day."

I hung up and contacted Mickey and the two PGA officials. The PGA men were in a panic. In all their years of overseeing golf tournaments, they'd never experienced anything like this. After discussing what they should do, they decided to telephone PGA headquarters in Florida for guidance. Management there told them to take charge, work with the police, coroner, etc. The PGA would notify the family.

Later that day, the sheriff showed up. He interviewed me for about thirty minutes, and I told them all that I could recall. The PGA officials provided more biographical details.

That afternoon the pro for whom Richard caddied arrived. When the PGA officials told him what had happened, he slumped into a chair. "I knew Richard was a recovering, binge alcoholic," he said with tears in his eyes. "In fact, he'd been doing quite well recently. We tour players have non-denominational religious services on Wednesday nights. Lately Richard has attended consistently with me."

To this day I wonder, what I could have done differently? Should I have stayed with him? Was there something I could have said to give him hope? I'll never know.

I'll always remember Richard Weaver, a young man whose demons were more than he could bear.

Epilogue

A year later, on Mother's Day, our telephone rang at home. Expecting it to be one of our children calling, I answered the phone. "Hello."

"May I speak with Rebecca Jordan?"

"This is she."

"Ms. Jordan, I'm Helen Weaver. Richard Weaver, the caddy who died in Mississippi last year, was my son. I have been told you were the last person to see Richard alive. Would you mind telling me about those final moments with him?"

Wow, out of the blue! I told her about the events and conversations we had prior to Richard's death. Having experienced a child's death myself, I understood her curiosity and pain. Sharing the information with Ms. Weaver was trying on me at the time, but she deserved to know the full particulars. Hopefully, knowing the details of the event will provide her some peace.

Author's Note: DEMONS

Alcoholics are the way they are, not merely by choice. They are diseased by this severe addiction. Studies have also revealed that alcoholism is hereditary.

Like many, the subject of this story could not resist the temptation. This nice-looking, hard-working, young man responded to his addictive curse.

Demons won an award in 2012 in a contest for Character Sketches from The Hot Springs Village Writers Club.

Whatever Happened to Harry

He used to be energetic
now he's listless
He used to be optimistic
now he's a pessimist
He used to be social
now he's a loner
He used to have friends
now he has few
He used to look to the present and future
now he looks at the past
He used to be physically strong
now he's weak
He used to be healthy
now he constantly has health problems
He used to be tolerant
now he's judgmental
He used to be busy
now he's often idle
He used to feel young for his age
now he feels old
He used to feel like a contributor
now he feels like a burden
He used to hear well
now he barely hears

He used to be active
now he sits in his chair
He used to be forgiving
now he carries a grudge
He used to be happy
now he's sad

WHATEVER HAPPENED TO HARRY?
HE'S GONE. I SURE MISS ME!

Author's Note: WHATEVER HAPPENED TO HARRY?

This story is a personal one. As I have grown older, I often lament on how life has changed. This is common to ponder as we realize advance age.

The ending reveals that many of the changes apply to me personally. Many people from audiences I have addressed have stated, "You could be talking about me."

Emancipation

Mona frowned. "Betty, what should I do?"

"About what?"

"There's a man who has bet with me almost everyday the last three weeks. He keeps asking me out to dinner."

"That's up to you. If you go out with him, you may enjoy yourself. If not, you can always make it the only time you go out with him. It's your call."

Mona and I are best friends. We work together as tellers at the racetrack. I'm happily married, but she is divorced.

"Ralph and I are having dinner Saturday night," Mona told me a few days later.

"That's great. I hope you have a good time."

"Well, how did it go?" I asked the following Monday.

A smile broke out on Mona's face. "It was a great evening. We're going out again Tuesday night."

Three weeks later Mona could not contain her excitement. "Look what Ralph gave me." She displayed a large ruby ring.

"Oh my goodness!" I gave her a hug.

"You're my best friend, so I'll tell you," she whispered in a hushed voice. "Ralph is moving in with me.

Isn't that exciting? He makes me so happy."

Several months passed. Then one day Mona asked, "Would you have a drink with me after work?"

"Sure."

After we were seated in a booth, tears came to her eyes. "Betty, Ralph seemed like all a girl could want, but now he's changed."

"In what way?"

"Well, he's not nearly as kind and affectionate as he used to be, and he now acts as if he owns me." Mona dropped her eyes and fidgeted with the ring on her finger.

"How does he act?"

"He forbids me from seeing my family." She looked up and frowned. "At first when one of them visited, Ralph left. He didn't want to meet them. Now, he gets mad if they even call me."

Uh oh. It's doubtful this attitude and these actions will go away. A control freak.

I patted Mona's hand. "Why don't you ask him to move out?"

"Well, I'm not sure what to do. He's never hit me, but he can get so angry!" Mona began to cry. "I just don't know. I can't go on like this."

A few days later I inquired, "Have you asked Ralph to leave?"

"He refuses to leave."

"Are you kidding me? It's your house!"

She merely shook her head. I could tell this was such a burden for my non-confrontational friend.

A couple of weeks later, she approached me again. "Betty, what would you do?"

"If it were me, I'd tell him he has one week to get out or I'll call the police."

Well, I'm happy to say that Mona finally screwed up her courage. She called the police, they evicted him, and a restraining order was issued.

Of course, Ralph went ballistic. He showed up at the racetrack and shouted profanities and slurs about her to everyone in earshot. It's a miracle he didn't shoot her or all of us! Her face reddened and she bowed her head to avoid eye contact with anyone.

In a further attempt to retaliate against Mona, Ralph wrote a letter to her employer suggesting she was a drug user. The employer asked if she would take a blood test. Of course, when she did, it was negative.

All of this has taken its toll. The change in Mona is obvious. By nature she is a quiet person. But now the hurt on her face never goes away. Often I can see the tears.

Because of his antics, an arrest order has been issued for Ralph. If he ever again sets foot in the state of Arkansas, he will be detained, Mona tells me. He still writes hateful letters to Mona, her mother, and her children. She tells me she never opens them. With all this in her recent past, Mona seems even more timid than before. She says she can't even think about dating men again.

One day she asked, "Betty, how did you meet such a nice man like Michael?"

I smiled. "There are plenty of them out there. You just haven't met the right one. Think of all the good times you had prior to meeting Ralph. There are more good times awaiting you."

"It's so hard."

"I know. But you're free now, dear friend. Just give it time."

Author's Note: EMANCIPATION

Emancipation is a true story. The names have been changed as a courtesy. The young lady who was the victim in this story, Mona, is very pretty. Besides being publicly embarrassed, she was devastated for quite a while. We have constantly reminded her that she has done no wrong and should feel no guilt.

John Walsh (of TV fame) mentioned in one of his books that he frequently encounters men whose motivation is to completely control and dominate lives of women. The Ralph in our story was such a fellow. He obviously was clever in how he won the affection of Mona, but over time he reverted back to his normal self.

I am pleased to report that some two years later Mona has returned to her normal, sweet self. To be sure, she is cautious but not fearful of men.

Garage Sale

Fred and Sharon are people of varied interests. Over the years they accumulated a variety of things, so they decided to hold a garage sale to sell the no longer wanted or needed items.

They offered to sell whatever their neighbors would want to include in the sale. Mickey Washington, a widow, had lovely offerings since she was finally downsizing her home. Mo Coffman had an extensive inventory of fishing paraphernalia. The Farners had been meaning to clean out their attic and garage, so this created a supply of merchandise.

A newspaper advertisement was arranged announcing the sale date and times. Signs were created to be placed at heavily traveled locations. A notice was posted on the church bulletin board.

The day before the beginning of the sale all merchandise was displayed and priced. A cashier's table was set up.

The turnout for the two-day sale was gratifying. Many people passed through their garage.

At sale's end a full accounting of the financial results was conducted. Counting total receipts, less payments to the respective neighbors and their personal purchases, Fred and Sharon had spent $38.75 more than they took in. Fred was overheard saying, "We cannot afford to have another garage sale."

Author's Note: GARAGE SALE

Our good friends and neighbors, the Swints, inspired this story. Every summer for the past nine years they have conducted a garage sale.

It seems every year it has resulted in similar success. A great deal of time performing the various duties, e.g. pricing the merchandise, arranging advertising in the local paper, soliciting other goods from the neighbors, creating and posting signs, setting up cashier's table (card table), and manning the site from early in the morning to dark for two days.

Despite all the planning, good intentions, and hard work, they usually conclude with deficit financial results. One must admire their enthusiasm.

"Garage Sale" won an award from The Fine Arts Center of Hot Springs in 2012.

Country Music

I can't tell you when my brother, Bobby Wolcott, developed his interest in music. It just was always around us when we grew up in Mayfield, Kentucky.

Our mother, Alice, played the piano. Most evenings after the dinner dishes were washed and dried, she played for a while. I can remember as a toddler Bobby would lie next to the piano while she played. Usually I was occupied elsewhere.

Barring some unusual event, the family ritual was to listen to the Grand Ole Opry from Nashville every Saturday night. We would sing along with the familiar songs and thrill to the sounds of the new ones.

On Sundays, Mother played the organ at church. We would sit in the first row and beam with pride at her talent and celebrity.

Bobby's musical indoctrination was accelerated on his tenth birthday. His gift from our parents was a shiny, new guitar. From that time on, the guitar was his frequent companion. When anyone couldn't locate Bobby, they knew to look for him on the front porch swing where he spent many hours picking his instrument and singing.

He made it a habit to save some of his three-dollar

allowance each week until he accumulated enough to buy sheet music of his favorite tunes. He taught himself how to pick and strum the guitar to achieve the desired sounds. If he could not afford new sheet music, he made up his own songs, both the melody and the lyrics. He would entertain himself by playing his creations.

As time passed, he improved as a picker. His voice was quite pleasant, and others asked him to sing a song just to hear him.

The junior high school conducted a program in which the students entertained their friends, parents, and other interested parties. The proceeds were to help fund the class trip. Without question, Bobby was the hit of the show and he performed two encores at the request of the audience.

During his senior year in high school, his friends and family encouraged him to enter the amateur talent contest at the Kentucky State Fair. To this day he will tell you that first place blue ribbon was one of the highlights of his life.

We have an uncle who was a member of Mayfield Country Club. After Bobby graduated from high school, Uncle Fred was able to secure a job for Bobby at the country club with the golf course maintenance crew. He spent most of the day driving a tractor pulling lawn mowers. He also raked sand traps, set up tee markers, moved golf holes, and performed any other task directed by the head greens keeper.

Since he was alone in the great outdoors, he often sang as he mowed. He continued to make up songs for his own enjoyment. He used to say, "I have the best of both worlds. By day I'm outdoors in the fresh air getting a golden suntan. In the evenings and on weekends I can play and sing music."

His reputation for his vocal ability was no secret in Mayfield, so he was offered a job on Friday and Saturday nights to sing at the Wagon Wheel. This establishment was quite popular, with a country and western flavor. It gave him the opportunity to practice and improve his voice control. He also expanded his repertoire of songs.

Bobby still lived with us at home. Aside from buying a used car, his bank account was growing. The automobile was not a beauty, lots of scratches and dents. It was mechanically sound, which is all he needed. He said, "As long as it gets me where I want to go."

After fifteen months or so the patrons at the Wagon Wheel, as well as his friends, suggested Bobby go to Nashville and take a shot at the "big time." They believed he had that much talent.

Bobby concluded, "Why not?" He had neither wife nor children, he had some seed money, and he had youthful time.

It was a rainy morning when he said good-bye to Mayfield and was Tennessee bound. Having done some advanced research, he drove to the James Robertson Hotel just off Broad Street. He was aware that the rates were moderate, and many of the stars initially called it home upon arriving in Nashville. In fact, Roger Miller was once a bellhop there, prior to becoming successful and famous.

The first night in town Bobby headed to the famous Tootsie's Tavern on Broad Street. This establishment is like a shrine to country and western fans, and is located just across the alley from the back exit to the original Grand Ole Opry building, Ryman Auditorium.

Many of the performers would slip out to Tootsie's for a beverage of their choice between appearances. Bobby said, "The lounge was just as I expected. The jukebox was blaring out country music. Every performer of note had autographed a picture to Tootsie, which covered the walls on all four sides."

Bobby found a stool at the crowded bar and struck up a conversation with three other young men. All three had recently come to Nashville from different states, mostly Southern, with a common goal. Each of them hoped to become discovered and ultimately achieve star status. The three of them shared an older home as their common residence.

"Would you like to move in with us and help share the expenses?"

"Sounds like a good idea to me." He welcomed the economy of the arrangement.

He began his efforts to get an audition by preparing a résumé of his vocal experience and accomplishments. He assembled a list of recording studios, agents, producers, and talent agencies. He sent each of these his flier and encouraged them to phone to set up an audition session. Unfortunately, he received no response. Obviously these folks were inundated with such appeals.

Next, he paid to have a demo tape made of him singing several songs. With one hundred copies, he decided to attempt personal solicitation.

Music Row is a six-block area with music-related businesses on both sides of the street, although at one time this was a residential area.

Bobby began his door-to-door visits like a Fuller Brush man, but he couldn't get past receptionists and administrative assistants. At each stop he left a demo tape along with his flier soliciting an audition opportunity.

Once again, his efforts were not rewarded. His finances were running low and he was becoming discouraged.

He called and asked, "Should I keep trying?"

We answered, "Yes."

Scanning the want ads in the Tennessean Sunday newspaper he responded to an ad seeking waiters at Luigi's Restaurante. Luigi's is acknowledged to be the finest Italian restaurant in the metropolitan area.

After being hired and trained, he was scheduled to work four nights a week, including the busy nights of Friday and Saturday. This still afforded him time to pursue his audition-seeking endeavors.

The compensation from his Luigi's employment was greater than he expected and was certainly needed. Since the restaurant was an upscale eatery with affluent patrons, they tipped generously.

He was tending to a private party of twenty-two on one occasion; thus he worked closely with the host and they developed a rapport. When Bobby learned the customer, a Mr. Farner, was affiliated with the music business, he asked Mr. Farner, "Could you help me get an audition?" Mr. Farner gave Bobby his business card and suggested if he would call the following week, an audition could be arranged.

In his naiveté Bobby didn't realize the good fortune of his accidental contact. Farner-Rea was one of the largest and more respected music production firms. Stan Rea, the legendary performer, and Mr. Farner were original founders. The person Bobby met was the son of the original Mr. Farner, and he was now one of the principals of the firm.

People he knew in the business advised Bobby not to sing songs at the audition that were already huge hits performed by stars. "They are not looking for clones," he was told. Rather he should perform to show off his uniqueness and his individual qualities.

The songs he chose to perform were three of those he had personally written, two love songs and a honky-tonk novelty number. I had heard him play and sing them many times. They were: "It Will Always Be You," "From Friend to Lover to Soul Mate," and "Party Hearty the Clock is Ticking."

After the audition, he was told that he would be called within a week, after the three people in attendance met to share their observations. True to their word, Bobby received a phone call four days later. He was told he had a fine voice but it lacked star quality, in their opinion. Having not heard the songs he performed previously, they asked, "Where did you get the songs you sang?" He replied that they were his own creations.

Being quite surprised, they suggested he should call a Mr. Steve Wershay at ABC Publishers who was the chief executive of the Nashville operation for this national firm. They alerted Mr. Wershay to expect his call.

Bobby's disappointment in the results of his voice audition bordered on devastation. Again, he called and said, "I'm coming home."

Mother again said, "Don't give up yet." He said he would follow up on the call to Mr. Wershay, but it was with meager anticipation.

On the arranged day Bobby arrived early with his guitar. After the introductions he was asked to sing the three songs he performed at Farner-Rea. The ABC people were overwhelmed. They asked, "Do you have any others?" He responded he did, but they were all in his head. Immediately, they offered him a contract to write songs. His excitement had his hand shaking so much he could barely sign his name on the contract.

Within ninety days one of the biggest country music stars recorded "It Will Always Be You." It became the number one hit in the country, and achieved platinum sales status.

Besides selling music for a lump sum, the greatest source of revenue for a songwriter is the royalties received every time the song is performed. The income stream from just one song can be enormous. With more than one thousand radio stations, all the jukeboxes in the country, all the live performers, the sale of CDs, records, and sheet music, there is tremendous exposure. He called home again and said, "My income worries are over."

From that point forward things improved decidedly. Now he was in high demand. Agents, studios, and performers were calling him regularly seeking new creations. He went from the pursuer to the pursued. Within thirteen months three of his songs were in the top fifty recordings.

While at an industry award party one night, he was introduced to Roxanne Gardner. Her blonde hair and light blue eyes completely mesmerized him. He later told me, "She is the most beautiful woman I have ever seen."

Roxanne was the lead singer in the Gardner Sisters vocal group. They often performed as the opening act to a major star's appearance. She was two years younger than Bobby's twenty-eight years.

They began an eight-month courtship. Besides her

ravishing looks, he was overwhelmed by her soft, laid-back approach to life. Nothing seemed to bother her, and she was a quick wit and had a hearty sense of humor.

She accepted his offer of marriage after they had met each other's families. Our family gave unanimous approval. The wedding was held in Nashville with a small number of their close friends. At the ceremony, she told me, "Don't worry, Willie, I'll take good care of him."

Today, some three years later, Bobby and Roxanne have a lovely five-bedroom home in Old Hickory, Tennessee. This suburb of Nashville is home to many of country music's top performers. Their home has Southern charm, with large white columns on three acres of lush green grass surrounded by a white picket fence.

Roxanne understands the demands of the music business. She and Bobby adore their one-and-a-half-year-old daughter, Becky, and spend much time playing with her.

Two signs hang prominently in their home. One at the entrance foyer reads, "Enjoy the Good Life." The other in Bobby's studio room is inscribed, "Remember Your Roots."

Bobby has stated. "Sometimes I have to pinch myself to realize what has happened. Perhaps some day I will write a song about it."

Author's Note: COUNTRY MUSIC

Having been raised in Nashville, Tennessee, I witnessed many young, aspiring songwriters, musicians, and performers. "Country Music " is fiction but it is very typical of these "wannabes."

Their profiles are talented, young people from small towns (usually). Most are from the South. They struggle to get the opportunity to be discovered. Some fail, some become studio musicians, and some go on to "fame." I know people in all categories.

Evolution

It was a day he had been eagerly anticipating for some time. Twenty-six months ago Patrick Murphy began working at the Palace Hotel. The hotel was an upscale, boutique, highly rated, three-diamond property. Patrick was its assistant general manager.

The general manager, Joe Clem, was a former classmate at the Premiere Hotel Management Institute. They shared a common base of professional knowledge.

Clem hired Patrick to create profits. The parent company, Armstrong Corporation, was getting much heat from the wealthy investors who owned the property.

Patrick was given responsibility for the Sales, Food and Beverage, and Catering Departments, all avenues that created revenue. In his first fourteen months, he increased the sales volume and cut the financial losses by thirty-five percent. In the most recent twelve months the operations performed just short of breaking even. Now he was headed for a performance review scheduled by Clem. He was confident a promotion, income raise, and/or a bonus were in the offing.

Leaning forward, hands folded on his desk, Clem

said, "The company has decided to implement an expense austerity program to increase profitability. True, the revenues have made significant improvement, but we need to slash expenses."

Then the general manager dropped the bomb. "Patrick, I am putting you on notice of your termination thirty days from now."

It was as if Mike Tyson had punched him in the stomach. He felt betrayed; he felt ill. Hadn't he vastly improved sales and revenue? How could Clem not point this out to the Armstrong leaders? The recent numbers of improvement should be obvious to anyone.

Disillusioned, confused, and angry, he was determined to consider a career change — one where he was the general manager with more employment stability.

Not long after he was terminated, Patrick encountered a former teacher from the Premiere Hotel Management Institute. He told Patrick, "Professor Jenkins just retired from the faculty and the school is seeking a replacement."

After several interviews, Patrick was hired. Of course, being an alumnus with practical experience made his resume more attractive.

Patrick's age, thirty-six, made it easy for students to identify with him. There was plenty of job security and stability. While his income was less, it was sufficient for one person to live an enjoyable lifestyle.

After three years of academia, Patrick yearned to return to the action. He was more mature and more knowledgeable. True to his prior commitment, he would only accept a position with a hotel as general manager.

He considered only those opportunities where his

identity could remain anonymous in the beginning. He would provide a confidential resume after he determined there was strong mutual interest.

After researching many opportunities, Patrick found three of particular interest.

He evaluated location, size, and type of property; facilities; income potential; and mission statement.

One opportunity stood out above the rest. He learned it was a hotel in an acceptable location with two hundred thirty rooms. It was an upscale operation that caught Patrick's eye. They were seeking a general manager to direct all operations.

After three face-to-face, in-depth interviews, an attractive offer was extended. Patrick refused to accept it without a binding three-year employment contract. The company agreed to the terms.

To protect the desired anonymity at both ends, it was agreed Patrick would give his thirty-day notice on a given morning. That same afternoon he would go to the property and meet its management team. He was told there was an assistant general manager with experience who would run the operation while he was winding up his affairs at the school.

On the designated day, all went as planned. Patrick tendered his resignation. He was escorted to a meeting room at the hotel where all the management team was assembled. On cue, Patrick walked in.

The secretary smiled. "Patrick Murphy, meet your assistant general manager, Joe Clem."

Author's Note: EVOLUTION

There is an old saying: "What goes around, comes around." This story is an excellent example of that. If there is a message, it should be treat everyone with kindness and respect, because you never know what the future holds.

The challenge that lies ahead is for Patrick and Joe to forge an effective, friendly relationship.

Almost Perfect

Being over 70 I'm often quizzed
As to how my health condition is.
I tell the asker, "Do not worry
To leave this earth I'm in no hurry."
Of course it's true I have two steel knees
But I can still get around as I please.
I eliminated my feet's woes
When they removed the ingrown nails from my toes.
Without my glasses I cannot read
But with Walgreen's specials I'm up to speed.
I'm grateful for the engineering
That gave me aids to boost my hearing.
My heart attack was very mild
But my five stents make me feel like a child.
Daily, I check my blood pressure
Just to be sure it is an acceptable measure.
Triglycerides and cholesterol I don't understand
But I take the pills to please the man.
To miss any meals I would certainly hate
Even to lose lots of excess weight.
So thanks again for your concern
I'll let you know if my health takes a turn.
Some people's lives become a mess
But I suppose I must be blessed.

Author's Note: ALMOST PERFECT

As I was preparing for a doctor's appointment not long ago, my wife helped me prepare a laundry list of problems to discuss with him. The list included aches and pains, as well as questions. A review of medications I take was also necessary.

That made me realize, over time, with age, my health had deteriorated. Inquiring of friends my age, I discovered they too had a depreciation in their health.

Since it is human nature to not admit to a slippage, "Almost Perfect" was written to highlight the sunny-side-up attitude as these things occur. Many folks have told me they can relate to this story.

Pigeon Poop

The mayor of San Francisco has a doctorate in urban planning. Terry Harding has studied traffic control, water utilization, municipal financial management, and police and fire department administration. Having been his administrative assistant for many years, I never dreamed his biggest challenge would be pigeon poop. It all started with a report in California Living.

"Loretta, have you seen this article on the best and worst of California?"

"Yes, your honor," I answered. "It seems to be the talk of the town."

"It must be, as we are being deluged with emails and telephone calls asking what we are going to do about it. The nerve of that guy saying pigeons in San Francisco are the number one problem in the state. See that this topic is on our agenda for the next council meeting."

I followed his instructions. When the meeting was conducted, there was a huge outcry. It seemed every council member was getting complaints from their constituents demanding something be done.

When tourism is your largest revenue producer, anything that diminishes it is taken seriously.

Furthermore, the money the tourists spend is a large part of our tax base.

The council all agreed that these pigeon droppings were a serious impediment to the city's tourism efforts. Since it was a nonpartisan issue — the pigeons do not discriminate — they considered it of primary importance that a solution to the problem be implemented. In response, the mayor mandated the following: "An ad hoc committee of three council members shall be appointed to study the problem and report back with a suggested solution. Councilman Frank Tinkers will serve as chairperson."

And so, the birds' falling waste was no longer ignored. The citizens could be advised that the situation was being dealt with. In other words, we could drop the subject of droppings.

"Hopefully, Loretta, we will soon have the feathered culprits under control. Frank Tinkers is a good man."

"He certainly is," I replied.

Committee Councilman Tinkers gave a report at the next meeting: "Mr. Mayor, we have considered a variety of options. It is our conclusion that the best thing for us to do is to periodically release a gas called peroxide uranium into the atmosphere over San Francisco. This substance, referred to as P.U., is so repugnant to birds that they will refuse to go where it exists."

"Sounds interesting. Write the legal department to ascertain if any laws would be broken. Tell them to reply to my office promptly."

After several weeks, Mayor Harding received a memo. There were no illegalities involved. Encouraged by this finding, a note was sent to the chamber of commerce for its input.

The chamber's leaders replied negatively. In their study of the matter, they were informed that releasing P.U. into the atmosphere would certainly eliminate the offending pigeons. However, there was no guarantee the substance wouldn't also permeate the entire area, not just the upper atmosphere. Thus the tourists would vanish along with the pigeons.

"You mean, Mr. Tinkers, your committee has had six weeks to look into the matter and this is the best you can come up with?"

"Yes, your honor."

"While we appreciate your effort, time is of the essence. To approach the matter from a different angle, I now appoint William Evers to chair the committee and he may select any two other council members to serve with him. At our next council meeting five weeks from now, Mr. Evers, we want to hear the strategy of your committee as to how to proceed and solve this matter."

Evers is a very conscientious person. Many nights, I saw him carry home reports to read, study, and research all aspects of the dilemma. Often the next day, his two committee members would meet with him to discuss the findings.

At the next council meeting, they reported: "After much consultation with the scientific community, we learned of a drug called NBM, an acronym for No Bowel Movement. Injections into the birds will cause severe constipation. It is contagious, so if we capture and administer the drug to one-third of the pigeon population, then turn them loose, soon we should realize a substantial drop in droppings."

"Then it's done. Good job, Mr. Evers. Please submit a written memo to the mayor's office spelling out precisely how this will be implemented and the expected results. And Loretta, after receiving that report, please release it to the public through all the usual publicity channels."

Things seemed to be resolved until the following Thursday morning.

"Mayor Harding, there is a Mrs. Payne on line one for you."

"Hello."

"This is Irma Payne, president of PETA. As you are aware, our national headquarters are here in San Francisco. Is the program regarding the pigeons described in yesterday's newspaper accurate?"

"Yes, it is."

"Do you realize the pain and suffering these helpless birds will experience if you inoculate them? It is inhumane. How would you like your children purposely getting a shot to cause constipation? Have you no compassion?

"If this plan of the city is not cancelled immediately, you will have more excrement to deal with than just the pigeons'. Next Monday morning, we will arrange to have ten thousand PETA members outside your office protesting this vicious behavior. We will see that it gets national publicity. Can you imagine the negative effect this will have on tourism by the millions of animal lovers? I will be watching for your withdrawal of the plan. Good day, sir."

"Loretta, please schedule an emergency council meeting for tomorrow morning."

Of course, in light of the PETA threat, the plan was scrapped and all media outlets notified. Talk about frustration. Mayor Harding was at his wit's end. I've never seen him so surly and short-tempered.

No alternative was available other than to make still another effort.

Once again, the ad hoc committee chairperson was changed. The most experienced person on the council, Lisa Chance, was approached and she accepted the chairmanship.

The first thing Chance did was ask for an increased budget to thoroughly research the assignment. The increase was granted. At various times, she traveled to Sacramento, the state capital, to meet with department heads there. She made two trips to Washington, D.C., to visit with federal agencies.

After three months, the mayor was notified the committee had completed its task. The council convened to hear the report: "After enormous effort, consultation, and study, we believe we have an acceptable program. The primary source of our proposal came from meetings with the U.S. Food and Drug Administration in Washington. They made us aware of a drug used in World War I while training the courier pigeons. It is introduced to birds in pellet form with their food. It is odorless and tasteless. The net result is they cannot procreate. It renders them sterile.

"While we could not find a lasting short-term solution, this should alleviate the problem in the long haul. Birth control leads to fewer births, which will greatly diminish the number of birds needing to relieve themselves. A slower but effective process."

Immediate relief was desired, but at least this seemed to be an ultimate problem-solver. Press releases were issued telling of the process to be utilized. An air of relief settled over the council.

It was a much more relaxed mayor who received a registered letter a week later. It was addressed to the Honorable Terry Harding. "I read of the program you intend to conduct to provide birth control pellets to the pigeons of San Francisco. As you know, the Catholic Church is opposed to all forms of birth control. Therefore, we request the city not offend the Catholic population, which represents a majority of your voting citizens." Reverend Joseph Vitale, Bishop of the Diocese of San Francisco, signed it.

I was in the room last week when, by a vote of nine to zero, the council tabled the topic. After the fall elections, they would let the newly elected council address the droppings problem.

As for my advice, if you are coming to San Francisco anytime soon, you can still ride the trolleys, you can still eat wonderful seafood at Fisherman's Wharf, you can still see the Giants play at Candlestick Park, but be advised you might be under attack by pigeon poop every step of the way.

One cannot say we did not try. After all, we appointed our most gifted leadership, from Tinkers to Evers, to Chance.

Author's Note: PIGEON POOP

One Sunday while reading the travel section of our newspaper, I read of a problem in San Francisco. It stated that pigeon droppings were having a significant, negative effect on tourism. Of course, the total revenue from tourism is very sizable.

The bizarre nature of this piqued my interest as a potential comedy short story. Developing the various obstacles truly entertained me.

At the end of the story there is reference to "Tinkers to Evers to Chance." The irony created was also reference to the initial baseball double-play combination. Even today baseball experts will recognize the names.

Pigeon Poop won an award at the 2013 Arkansas Writers Conference.

The Unknown

While I was alive, I used to hear people say, "That's the way I want to go, alive one minute and gone the next. No suffering, hospital bills, or grief to others." I would nod my approval.

I now feel differently. During my last minutes on earth family, my wife, children, and grandchildren surrounded me. I heard all of them tell me good-bye and hug and kiss me. Being with all of those I dearly loved on earth gave me a great deal of satisfaction. I was proud of the legacy I was leaving behind.

Departing from the human world was both an ending and a beginning. My humanity had ended. But my future was still uncertain.

All that exists now is my soul. I require no food, water, or other nourishment to exist. I reside in an environment of constant brilliant light.

There is no sense of time. There is no day or night. There is no week, month, year. I do not know how long my soul has been in its present state or will remain so. I exist in a constant, neutral environment. I assume there will be a final destination, but I know not where or when.

Having lived primarily a charitable and moral life,

I have no fear regarding my last journey. Besides, there is nothing I can do about it now.

Some questions occur to me. Will I be able to identify my parents? My former friends and relatives? Will there be any form of dialogue among us? Will a complete state of euphoria exist to be joyfully experienced by one's self? Once I arrive at my eternal resting place will I be able to observe my living friends and relatives on earth as they conduct their lives?

I used to wonder and think about life after death. To all earthly human beings it remains a mystery, yet one's soul must keep the faith. There is more to come.

However, the idea of eternity is difficult to comprehend. Existence without end is a new reality. I suppose until I experience it, I will not fully understand it.

Human experience on earth is a teacher. Past actions create a memory bank of how activities unfold and result. There are no past experiences in the afterlife. Any and all functions are new.

Perhaps my curiosity should scare me to death, but then that would be redundant, wouldn't it?

Author's Note: THE UNKNOWN

At some time in our lives everyone ponders what happens to us when we die. This story addresses one possible scenario. It is not based on science. It is not based on religion. It is merely a speculation by the author. I hope it stimulates the readers to consider their own beliefs.

A Tribute to Moms

It's amazing how many feelings one can experience in a few, short moments. Such was the case of Rebecca McCormack. As she sat in the audience watching the collegiate graduation ceremonies of her youngest son, Craig, she felt relief, pride, and curiosity.

Her relief was understandable, as she had spent the past seventeen years being the sole provider and caregiver for her two sons. With Craig's graduation, both he and his older brother, Michael, who previously received his college degree, were now capable and equipped to take total charge of their lives. They could pursue their own dreams and ambitions as they chose.

Difficult as it was to recall, it was when Craig was five that Rebecca divorced and was granted custody of the children. She was aware that little or no responsibility for the boys, financially and emotionally, could be expected from their father.

To be sure, her past seventeen years had been challenging. Sometimes it bordered on overwhelming. She had to be creative. Meals often consisted of extreme budget restrictions, with items such as macaroni and cheese, grilled cheese sandwiches, and the like. Activities for the boys were created to minimize expenses. Trips to the City Park and playground were frequent. The public library provided a plethora of free activities. Despite past trials, both her boys always felt loved, which they were, and responded to her parental leadership. Yes, there existed a feeling of relief that they traveled the past together and not only survived but succeeded.

How could Rebecca not experience pride? The achievements of Michael and Craig were a testament to their character and industry. Despite some sacrifices, fewer toys, modest clothes, and other amenities, they never felt slighted. Teaching, providing leadership by example, and consistently attending church, provided a basic core of values and morals.

Perhaps Rebecca's greatest source of pride was her unwillingness to become a welfare participant. Her income level qualified her for public assistance despite the fact that she worked two jobs for much of the time. Not depending on charity or others to meet her responsibility never was truly an option to this proud mother.

Having traveled this road for such a period of time, her life was about to move in another direction. While she would forever love her children, she could focus on and wonder what lay ahead for her. Her curiosity was piqued.

Caring for her own wants and needs would become more primary. Tending to her own education and career ambitions could now be addressed. At a still young age, 42, and quite attractive, she certainly would attract some suitors. In the past this was a minor consideration in her life. What the future now held was not a given but the possibilities were intriguing.

With all these reflections in her memory, Rebecca smilingly concluded, "Life is good."

Author's Note: A TRIBUTE TO MOMS

As a curious observer of our communities and our cultures, one conclusion has been drawn. The most dedicated and heroic people, in my opinion, are the single parent, working moms.

They must raise the children daily (clean them, clothe them, feed them, transport them to school or nursery, retrieve them afterwards, arrange some play time, feed them again, supervise their homework, prepare for tomorrow).

Aside from all these tasks they must find and hold a responsible job. How in the world do they do it?

"A Tribute to Moms" is a fictitious story of such a woman who made the sacrifice successfully. Her pride and feelings at that journey's end are most admirable.

A Phone Call to Love

Rebecca

It was not a joyful time in her life. She had been divorced from her former husband for ten months. Somehow, they just couldn't find the happiness they each sought from their marriage.

It must have been more evident to others than to Rebecca. She remembered her brother asking her as they drove to the wedding rehearsal, "Are you sure you want to do this? You both are so different." Her husband had an accountant's somber demeanor, and she possessed a friendly, outgoing personality.

Perhaps they had married too young. At the time it didn't seem impulsive. In retrospect, it probably was. Neither had an established career, so from the beginning they could barely get by financially. As time passed it seemed there was even less time for each other's needs.

Now she had some fears about what the future might hold. The past years provided some stability and security, but there was no excitement, no challenge. Life was too routine and showed no sign of ever changing. She regretted having to end the marriage, but she wanted more from life.

So, it was in this frame of mind that she answered the telephone for her boss, Ken Thomas. She had been his executive secretary for almost a year, and they worked very well together.

"Mr. Thomas' office."

"May I please speak to Ken?"

"I'm sorry, Mr. Thomas is in a meeting and cannot take your call."

"Just tell him it is Michael Gordon. He will take my call."

Rebecca again informed Mr. Gordon of Mr. Thomas's unavailability. He insisted she inform Ken who was calling.

Boy, he sure thinks he's a big shot. You would think he would take no for an answer.

"Mr. Thomas, there is a rude person on the phone named Michael Gordon who insists you will take his call."

"I'll take his call; he's a great guy."

Rebecca was not thrilled to put the call through but obeyed. She hoped he wouldn't call again.

Three weeks later Michael called again.

"Rebecca, may I please speak to Ken?"

"I'm sorry, but he's in a very important meeting."

"This is somewhat of an emergency. One of our best friends had a heart attack while we were on convention in Germany. I've just returned to the USA with the body and widow."

She put Michael on hold. After knocking, she entered the conference room and whispered the information in Ken's ear. He immediately rose and headed for the telephone.

"Michael, what happened?"

"Ernie Cooper had a heart attack and didn't make it."

"My God!" Ken gasped. "Not Ernie. What can I do to help?"

"I'll call later and give you the funeral details. Carol is so distraught and Ernie's son, Tim, is not in much better shape. I'll assist with the arrangements."

"Tell Carol I love her. Let me know if you need me for anything."

Upon hanging up, Ken stated to Rebecca, "Michael is really a big-hearted guy." With that Ken headed for his office with tears in his eyes and closed his door.

Fifteen minutes later Michael called once more. "Rebecca, is Ken okay?"

"He's very upset. What happened?"

"We were celebrating the tapping of a keg of beer and doing a snake dance to the German oom-pah music. Ernie Cooper stopped, grabbed his chest, and fell to the ground. He was dead when he hit the floor. Carol, his widow, screamed and I got her out of the party room. I am calling from JFK airport in New York. We are between flights. I'm taking Carol and the body to Columbus."

This Michael may not be such a bad guy after all.

For the next eight months, Rebecca and Michael spoke often. Whenever he called to talk business or football with Ken, which was quite often, they had pleasant, friendly conversations. As time passed she found Michael quite interesting and entertaining. Also, if Mr. Thomas was so complimentary of Michael, she reasoned, he must be okay. One could say she became intrigued by Mr. Gordon.

Michael was invited to attend a business meeting in Dallas. He called Rebecca. "Would you have dinner with me one evening while I am in town?" She agreed. "Select one of your favorite restaurants and make reservations. I'll be stopping by Ken's office and will see you there."

She asked, "What do you look like?"

He responded, "I am a stocky, red-faced Irishman."

On the day of his arrival, Rebecca was filling in for the receptionist on their floor while the receptionist was at lunch. Shortly after noon a gentleman got off the elevator and approached her. "I'm here to see Mr. Thomas."

She immediately knew who he was, so she introduced herself and said, "Well, you didn't lie." He was stocky and of ruddy complexion. He was very well dressed and had a confident air about him, and she could sense he was comfortable in a leadership position. They confirmed the evening's plans.

She picked up Michael at his hotel at 7:00 p.m. and they drove to a fine Italian restaurant. They ordered a bottle of wine and visited quite a while before ordering dinner. After a wonderful meal, another bottle of wine was ordered. They lost track of time because they were absorbed in learning more about each other. Rebecca would remember it as "the most romantic dinner date she had ever experienced."

She drove him back to his hotel. He gave her a simple good night kiss. "I'll be back in touch." She drove home wondering if she would ever see him again. She hoped so.

Michael

It was to be a routine telephone call to an old friend of twenty years. Ken Thomas and Michael Gordon had much in common. They were close to the same age, they both were in the insurance business, and as ex-athletes they both were sports fans. Ken had graduated from the University of Oklahoma and Michael from the University of Tennessee.

At this point in his life, Michael was preoccupied with his work. He owned and managed an independent financial services firm with four offices, fifty-two representatives, and seven administrative employees.

His personal life seemed nonexistent. He lived alone in a lovely condominium overlooking Lake Michigan in downtown Milwaukee. He was the type of person who thrived on activity. He did not like being alone. He went to work early and came home late to his empty abode. Was he busy? Yes. Was he lonely? For sure.

The telephone call was placed, and Ken's secretary, who obviously was requested to hold his calls, refused to put Ken on the line. After much insistence, Michael finally persuaded her to personally ask Ken if he would take the call. When he agreed to speak with Michael, it was apparent it irritated Ms. Miller. The pleasantness in her voice subsided.

After getting off to a strained start, the Rebecca Miller – Michael Gordon relationship became friendly, cordial, and in time, very pleasant. Michael wondered if she was as delightful in person as she was on the telephone. Her voice had a sparkle to it like a twinkle in an eye.

"What does she look like, Ken?"

"She is very attractive and available."

This, of course, elevated Michael's interest.

They became phone pals similar to pen pals. They spoke from time to time, and his curiosity and interest grew. He often called to learn that Ken was out of town on business. Often Michael welcomed that, as it gave him more opportunity to talk with Rebecca.

When it became necessary for Michael to attend a meeting in Dallas, he saw an opportunity to finally meet Rebecca personally. Rebecca accepted his invitation to have dinner with him while he was in Dallas. He was looking forward to the evening with great anticipation and enthusiasm.

He mentioned he would see her at her office earlier that day and asked, "What do you look like?"

She said she was five feet, four inches tall, and had short, dark brown hair. Ken had already briefed him regarding her appearance, of course. Ken's exact words were, "She's a fox."

When Michael got off the elevator on the eighth floor, he approached the receptionist. "Where will I find Ken Thomas' office?"

"You are Michael Gordon, aren't you?" She introduced herself as Rebecca Miller. Michael thought, "Boy! Was Ken right. She is lovely." After they discussed arrangements for their dinner date that evening, Michael proceeded to Ken's office for the meeting. It was very difficult to keep his mind on business. His thoughts kept drifting back to Rebecca. She has beautiful eyes. Large and very dark. He had always looked at a woman's eyes to judge her beauty.

As agreed, Rebecca picked up Michael, and they drove to the restaurant. As she drove, Michael could not take his eyes off her. As she drove she hiked her long skirt up to her knees so she could manipulate the foot pedals. Her shapely legs seemed to dominate the entire front seat.

After being seated, Michael asked, "What is your favorite wine?"

"Chardonnay."

A bottle was ordered. The conversation focused on themselves, sharing a synopsis of their lives, their likes and dislikes. It was evident that thus far neither had achieved what they sought in life. Their similarities were recognized by both of them. Both shared religious beliefs, had a quick sense of humor, and were optimistic by nature. He thought, where has she been? This is like the butterfly story. One can chase what they desire to no avail. When he sits down to rest along comes what he wants and sits on his shoulder. Rebecca seemed to be what he was seeking.

After dinner he could not bring himself to leave. He wanted to spend as much time with her as possible. "Waiter, bring us another bottle of wine, please." The conversation continued.

She drove Michael to his hotel. He thanked Rebecca. "I'd like to see you again."

"I'd like that."

The next day at the airport he arranged for a dozen yellow roses to be delivered to her at her office with a card expressing thanks for an amazing evening.

Together

Both Rebecca and Michael reflected often on their

dinner date. They could not have scripted a better beginning. They were relaxed, comfortable, and it was more fun than either of them had experienced in a long time. In fact, on that occasion they both began to have thoughts of love.

They began exchanging telephone calls three or four times a week. Michael gave Rebecca his toll free number and encouraged her to call. After several weeks of this Michael suggested they get together for a weekend.

The Hyatt Hotel chain was conducting a promotion directed to executive secretaries. Every time a secretary booked her boss's reservations with Hyatt, she received bonus points towards a free night's lodging. Rebecca accumulated enough for three free nights.

Together they decided on a weekend. Rebecca was to fly to Chicago Thursday night and return to Dallas Sunday afternoon. Chicago was chosen because American Airlines had a direct flight there, and it was merely a one-hour drive from Milwaukee for Michael. She made a reservation at the Watertown Hyatt in downtown Chicago.

"I'll pick you up outside the baggage claim area. I'll be driving a black Cadillac," Michael told her.

When she arrived he was waiting as planned. Her first words were, "I thought you were joking about the black Cadillac." Rebecca signed in at the registration desk at the hotel while Michael stood behind her holding her two pieces of luggage.

The clerk inquired, "Who is he?"

Michael quickly replied, "I'm her bodyguard." They all got a chuckle out of that.

It wasn't the baseball game or the theatre or the music in Rush Street establishments that highlighted the weekend — it was just enjoying each other's company.

While strolling the "Miracle Mile," which is a five-block area of some of the finest stores in America, Michael spied a dress in the window of Gucci's. "Boy, that dress would look terrific on you. Let's go in and you can try it on." They entered the store and Rebecca rather reluctantly tried on the dress. When the sales lady wasn't looking, Rebecca shook her head. They returned outside.

"Why didn't you like the dress?"

She gave a five-word answer, "Seven hundred and fifteen dollars." He understood and appreciated her practicality.

The extent of their passion for each other when they made love was an exhausting joy. It exceeded any previous experiences. Rebecca thought, he is such a thoughtful lover, not just interested in his own satis-faction. As for Michael, he was overwhelmed. I never thought at age fifty anyone could arouse me so often, and with so much intensity. It was obvious to both that they didn't just have sex — they made love.

Before Rebecca boarded her return flight, they agreed to see each other every other weekend. They would alternate travels. One weekend Michael would fly to Dallas, and two weekends later Rebecca would fly to Chicago. This arrangement was followed for several months. They traveled like this so often that the flight attendants got to know both of them on a first-name basis.

One Saturday night in Chicago, they enjoyed a delightful candlelight dinner at the famous Cape Cod Room in the Drake Hotel. Then Michael asked a seri-ous question. "At the rate we are going, AT&T and

American Airlines are getting rich. If we are ever to get together permanently, one of us has to relocate for a trial cohabitation period. I'm afraid it can't be me because I have to oversee my business, but will you join me in Milwaukee?"

Rebecca understood the proposal but wanted to give it some thought. There was quite a bit involved. It would be necessary to resign from my position, move away from friends and relatives, and reside in a community where I know no one. A move to Milwaukee from Dallas was over one thousand miles and not just around the corner.

The following week Rebecca responded. "I will consider moving to Milwaukee on three conditions: I can visit Milwaukee first to look it over; you will arrange to fly to San Antonio to meet my parents; and if either of us wants to terminate the relationship, we can do so with no questions asked." Michael agreed. If they didn't have a trial union, they would probably regret it the rest of their lives.

Rebecca took four days' vacation and flew to Milwaukee. She visited Michael's office building; the Regency Condominiums where he resided; many of the sights in town, like Brewer Baseball Stadium, the Performing Arts Center, Merrill Hills Country Club where Michael was a member; and many fine restaurants. She had an opportunity to meet some of Michael's friends, all of whom were friendly and likeable. She was satisfied.

Several weeks later Michael met Rebecca in San Antonio. Since Rebecca was thirty years old, she did not need her parents' consent but wanted to pay them the courtesy of meeting this man whom she had not known too long and who was nineteen years older than she. The four of them had a gourmet dinner at the Fig Tree Restaurant on the River Walk, a restaurant acknowledged to be among the finest dining places in San Antonio. Waterford crystal water glasses accented this point. Ken Thomas recommended the restaurant to Michael. Neither Rebecca nor her parents had ever eaten there.

The gathering was pleasant and cordial. Her parents still were concerned about her moving so far away but acquiesced to Rebecca's judgment.

Jointly they set a date for Michael to fly to Dallas to drive Rebecca's minivan to Milwaukee with her and her personal belongings.

Rebecca met with Ken Thomas. "I'm giving my two weeks' notice of resignation."

"You're going to Milwaukee, aren't you?"

"Yes, I am."

As soon as she left his office, he telephoned Michael. "Damn it, Gordon, you stole the best secretary I've ever had." Of course, he wasn't too surprised.

Rebecca wanted to have her own condominium in the Regency complex. She felt, at least at first, it might pacify her parents, so Michael arranged for her to occupy the unit just above his. It was extravagant paying two rents, but in the total scheme of things, a small price to pay.

After two months she joined Michael in his unit. This reinforced their attraction to each other. Every day was a joy. Awakening each morning with the sunrise reflected on Lake Michigan created a beautiful beginning to each day. Despite his continued hectic work schedule and her newness to the area, they were quite content just being in each other's company. It became apparent that what they had was not just a passing infatuation.

After four more months of living together Michael stated, "Let's make our relationship permanent by getting married." Her reply was, "I thought you would never ask." Michael presented her with an unusual, handmade diamond ring. Rebecca informed her family and flew to San Antonio to make arrangements.

The ceremony was held at a large suite at the San Antonio Hyatt Hotel on the River Walk. In attendance were a small gathering of close friends and relatives. Rebecca was beautiful in her wedding gown. She looked like an angel and her joyful smile radiated the room.

They honeymooned for four days in Lake Tahoe and then flew to Tahiti for one week to attend a convention trip Michael had earned because of the amount of business his company produced in the previous year. Since they had not informed the other attendees in advance, their marriage took everyone by surprise. Many of Michael's close business acquaintances met Rebecca for the first time. Although a bit overwhelmed, she quickly charmed them all. Of course, Michael was accused of "robbing the cradle."

After being married eight months they decided to buy a house. They selected one in a bedroom community adjoining Milwaukee. It was not a pretentious property but very comfortable and appealing on a well landscaped lot. Of course, they furnished the home to Rebecca's taste. The house became their home. They enjoyed entertaining others and hosting friends often.

Life settled down to more of a normal routine thereafter. Rebecca assisted with some administrative duties and took over the checkbook and paying the bills, business and personal. Between the payroll, commissions, and expenses of four offices, this was no small task. They enjoyed attending the theatre and sporting events, and Rebecca even took up golf, one of Michael's hobbies. Since they both enjoyed traveling, they visited places around the world as well as many parts of the United States. One would think they would get tired of each other, but that was not the case.

Their lives began anew on a day when a persistent Michael had to convince an irritated Rebecca to accept his telephone call to Ken Thomas.

Author's Note: A PHONE CALL TO LOVE

This story embraces many conditions and emotions. It begins with conflict and progresses to friendship. Thereafter it enters into romance, and then develops into love. Finally, a lifetime commitment is the result.

Rebecca and Michael experienced a variety of challenges and roadblocks. Their love for each other was so strong it prevailed ultimately.

Ecclesiastical Dilemma

This is my least favorite duty of being a priest. Every Saturday from 2:30 to 4:30 I hear confessions. It's always busy the first half hour. From 3:00 to 4:30 it's slow and boring. Oh well, it gives me a chance to pray and read. Oh, oh, someone just entered the confessional.

"It's been over two years since my last confession, but Father John, this is Clifford Graham. I've done a terrible thing."

"Tell me about it, my son."

"I'm unemployed and have a family to support. Last week I decided to rob a convenience store for some groceries to feed my kids. I wore a ski mask. After I entered the store, the clerk bent down. I thought he was going for a gun, and I instinctively shot him. You may have read about it in the papers. I didn't mean to harm anyone and took the gun only to get the employees to cooperate. The clerk died. For these and all my sins I am sorry."

I was stunned, and I paused for a moment to reflect on the severity of what I had just heard.

"I cannot give you absolution because of the gravity of your sin. I can only give you conditional absolution. Your sins will be forgiven if you meet these conditions. First you must make a firm resolution to never commit acts like these again."

"I will not, never, ever, so help me God."

"Secondly, some form of restitution must be made. Once you have become employed, set up a system to send the deceased's family a monthly amount anonymously for the rest of your life. I suggest at least fifty dollars. This is to remind yourself of the enormity of the event and to remind you to never repeat it." I paused again, but there was no response.

"Finally, I want you to pray the rosary daily for the next thirty days, asking the Lord for forgiveness. Now, say the Act of Contrition, sincerely expressing your remorse."

I had never been privy to knowledge of this magnitude. My conscience struggled. Was I fair? Did I provide any comfort?

Three weeks later I picked up the newspaper, and my distress grew. Bold headlines declared, "Killer of Convenience Store Manager Under Arrest." The article further stated, "Two patrons of the store have identified a 32-year-old as the shooter." It continued, "Despite the partial face cover, they had no doubt that James Reily, a previously convicted felon, was the shooter."

Oh no! Now what am I do? On the one hand I must honor my sacred vow to never reveal the details of a confession. However, it appears an innocent man could wrongfully lose his life.

As time went on I became more irritable. I lost my appetite. In fact, I lost twelve pounds. I was no longer the patient John Murphy I had always been. I decided to visit with my pastor, Monsignor Tohill, without revealing the confessor's identity.

"Father John, how are you?"

"Fine, Monsignor, but I have a serious problem, and I don't know what to do."

"Tell me about it."

"Recently, I heard the confession of one of our parishioners. Someone you and I know. He confessed to having committed a murder. He did not intend to kill anyone, but it was a murder, just the same. I read in the newspaper that someone else had been arrested for the murder."

Monsignor Tohill gasped, and I continued. "The prosecuting attorney said he might ask for the death penalty. The seminary never taught us how to deal with this type of conflict."

The Monsignor's eyes met mine and he nodded. "I can understand your agony. In forty years as a cleric I have never experienced what you described."

"What should I do?"

"The gravity of this is such that I feel we have to take the matter to a higher authority. I will contact the diocese for guidance. I'll request a meeting with the bishop."

A week passed and an appointment was arranged.

Monsignor Tohill and I were led into the bishop's office. As you can imagine, I was very nervous.

"Thank you, Bishop O'Hare, for meeting with Father John and me."

"You're quite welcome, Monsignor. Any time. Have a seat. What can I do for you?"

"Father John recently heard the confession of a man, whom he recognized, who admitted having committed a murder. An innocent person has been arrested for the crime. He may be given the death penalty.

What is Father John to do?"

The bishop grimaced, paused, and then said, "This is a very serious matter, as you stated. It will require some thought, prayer, and counsel. I cannot give you an answer at this time. I will get back to you." He had a blank expression and appeared very distressed.

On the drive back to the church, it was all I could do to fight back the tears. Both the monsignor and I were quiet.

What would Jesus do? He would not want a sacred vow broken. But he would not want an innocent man put to death. This was driving me crazy. John, you may not be able to resolve this without help.

Ten days later Monsignor Tohill and I were summoned to the bishop's office. As we entered, I thought I saw a grim look on the bishop's face.

"I researched the matter. In the history of the diocese this is an unprecedented event. I serve on several community committees with the district attorney. We have become friends. Without revealing the confessor's name, which I do not care to know, I outlined our confidential knowledge in this matter."

The bishop leaned forward as if he wanted to be certain we understood what he was about to say. "Several days later the district attorney called me back. He told me they only wanted to prosecute those who were guilty. In the normal course of business he assigns one of his staff to investigate a case, conduct the necessary interviews, and report the findings and recommendations to him, but this time he personally scrutinized all the facts of this case. What he learned astounded him.

"He said that one of the arresting officers was wired with a recorder at the time of the arrest. It revealed that Mr. Reily was not read his Miranda rights, nor offered an opportunity to contact an attorney. So, according to the law, Mr. Reily cannot be arrested or prosecuted. They'd have no choice but to drop the charges and release him. Father John, your confidential knowledge will remain confidential." The bishop smiled.

I felt like a balloon whose air was being released.

Monsignor Tohill stated, "Bishop O'Hare, we sincerely thank you. Your kind intercession has solved our problem and relieved Father John of his agony."

"You're welcome. Glad we could resolve the matter and maintain the integrity of the confessional."

As we left the room, I smiled and thought to myself, God certainly does work in mysterious ways.

Author's Note: ECCLESIASTICAL DILEMMA

Realizing that Catholic priests make a sacred vow to not publicly disclose any dialogue discussed in the confessional, I often considered the problem this could create in certain circumstances. I sought and received input from a Catholic priest friend of mine regarding the conflict.

This story is fiction but illustrates the very real possibility. The challenge was how not to penalize the distraught father who had true contrition but not prosecute the falsely accused.

It took me some time to contemplate such a solution.

Travel Tales

Preface

When I was a toddler, my mother and three other housewives/mothers of youngsters had an arrangement. Mondays through Thursdays they would rotate babysitting responsibilities for all of us children.

On one particular occasion my mother had arrived at her friend's house to collect me. I was nowhere to be found. Everyone searched high and low for twenty minutes. Finally, I was located. I had crawled into the pantry. The door had closed behind me. There I sat, perfectly content, my face covered with flour. I had spilled it all over the floor. Mother said I looked like a little snowman.

I tell that story because I believe it reveals the beginning of my lifelong love of traveling. Even then, I preferred to travel and "wing it" along the way.

Since then I have taken many trips, not as part of my career but for personal enjoyment. Many unscheduled events have occurred along the way. I will share several of them from different countries. More could be cited, but the following are examples of some of the many memorable moments my wife and I have experienced.

France

Becky and I exchanged homes for six weeks with a couple from Danmarie in the Alsace region of France. Dannemarie is a small town in the eastern part of France, bordering on Germany.

The couple at whose home we stayed had an automobile for our use. However, they had no garage. They had an arrangement with a neighbor across the street to lease a parking spot behind the neighbor's house in a small field of hers.

After seeing us come and go for several weeks, the neighbor's curiosity about "us Americans" got the best of her. One Saturday morning as we headed for our parked auto, she stepped outside and introduced herself as Madam Picah. She invited us into her home for some "tea."

Upon entering we were introduced to her brother from Paris and a sister and her husband. Madam Picah was a widow. It became obvious they were all visiting Madam Picah with the hope of meeting us. The thought of tea quickly was relinquished to glasses of wine. At 9:30 in the morning!

We learned the brother was an active part of the resistance movement in Paris during World War II. The other relatives shared interesting stories. Madam Picah was the most intriguing though. As a Jewess, she had been a prisoner at the notorious Auschwitz Concentration Camp. She still bore her permanently tattooed number on her forearm.

We invited Madam to dinner at our house the following evening and she accepted.

She walked across the street carrying an unlabeled, clear bottle of liquid. She explained it was schnapps made from a three-generation-old recipe. A later sip of it was a warming experience, to say the least. It must have been 90% alcohol. You could have removed wallpaper with it.

We spent the evening listening to this fascinating woman. She stated Dannemarie was taken over by the Germans during the war and she became a prisoner. During the early part of World War II a German officer and his family occupied the house in which we were residing.

"Did the German soldiers sexually assault you female prisoners?" I asked.

"Oh no, they wouldn't touch us. They considered us animals, not humans." She added, "The prisoner trustees were crueler than the Germans to gain the Germans' approval."

When the prison camp was liberated and the prisoners freed, it presented Madam a dilemma — how to return to her home. A nice captain in the American army wrote a letter to take with her. It explained she was a POW returning to her home. She still has the letter.

After a grueling trip, she found her house half destroyed by bombs. The house we lived in was not harmed at all, which was just a coincidence. Fate determined which properties were destroyed and which were saved during the bombing raids.

We shall never forget that strong woman. Madam Picah was a living history lesson.

I have often heard people say, "The French are not nice to Americans." This simply is not true. By nature they are not too friendly to anyone. Perhaps I should say they are private people. As an example, Madam Picah had never been in the house where we stayed although she had resided across the street from her neighbor for over forty-five years.

One morning after breakfast, at approximately ten o'clock, there was a knock at the door. I opened the door to reveal a gendarme. He asked if I spoke French (in French). I replied, "No."

I asked if he spoke English (in English). He responded, "No."

Then through a series of gestures he wanted to know who I was and what I was doing there. He pointed to the pile of mail on the kitchen counter. I knew just enough to say, "Chateau exchange." He nodded and understood.

After staying for three weeks, a next-door neighbor reported us for taking mail from the mailbox. We wondered why the three-week wait to report it? Why not come next door and inquire of us themselves? Such is the way of French people.

China

On a trip to Hong Kong, we took a side tour with a group into Red China. We stood in a line of approximately forty people for entry documentation check in. Standing in the area where we waited were two Chinese soldiers with machine guns draped around their heads at the ready.

In my playful (and stupid) way, I mumbled in an audible volume, "Mao Tse-tung sucks." After several of these mumbles my wife was about to kill me, and there were giggles and chuckles.

Hearing the sounds, one of the soldiers walked back to where we stood in line. He had a very somber, stern look on his face.

As he stood next to me I removed an expensive cigar from my coat pocket and offered it to him. He quickly looked it over and looked around to see if any of the other soldiers were in the area. When he saw none, he snatched it from my hand and quickly put it in his pants pocket, out of sight. Finally, he smiled at me and strolled away.

I tell this little story for it confirms my general belief. It does not matter where you are; if you treat people nicely they generally will treat you pleasantly in return.

Scotland

Two events we'll never forget occurred in Scotland. The first happened on Oran Island. We arrived at this small, seaside town without reservations. We located the only hotel/restaurant.

As we checked in, the lady clerk told us, "If you intend to have dinner with us, you better make your reservations and show up early." We peered in the dining room and noted it was empty and only seated approximately twenty patrons.

We thought she was kidding.

We went down for dinner around 5:30 and were

the only diners there. We chose a table by a window that looked out over a cove of water.

As we enjoyed our second cocktail, the nose of a submarine emerged from the water followed by the rest of the vessel. We were flabbergasted. Neither of us had ever witnessed a submarine this close, much less see it surface.

Shortly after it rose, some men emerged from the deck hatches. They climbed over the side and into motorized rubber rafts. Approximately four rafts with four sailors in each headed towards us.

We later learned that it was an English sub that had been patrolling the North Sea. They had dinner reservations for the officers, commissioned and non-commissioned.

Now the dining room was almost at capacity with sixteen sailors, Becky (the only woman), and me. Believe me, we got plenty of attention and free drinks.

We also experienced another interesting happenstance in Scotland. After driving for almost a full day, we did not want to go directly to bed. We asked the bed-and-breakfast proprietor where would be a good place to get a few drinks and hear some music.

Although it was only a mid-sized city, we were told there were a few places. The closest he recommended was a roadside structure out in the country. When we entered the place we were shocked. This joint was jumping! There must have been seventy-five people there. The music was blaring. Everyone was seated at wooden type picnic tables.

We took our seats at the only available one we saw. At the table with us were four Japanese gentlemen. After we had a few beers one of those men and I attempted to communicate. I pointed to my wife and said, "Becky."

I pointed to myself and said, "Mickey."

He nodded that he understood. Then he introduced himself and his companions. I have never heard so much multi-syllable gibberish. I nodded also.

I inquired by homemade sign language what were they doing in Scotland. He raised both arms, stretched them out, and twisted his wrists back and forth while he made a sound like he was repeatedly clearing his throat. We eventually figured out he was emulating a motorcycle. They were engineers working at the huge Honda factory in Scotland.

He asked a question I could not understand. Then he showed us a picture of his family. We did likewise and that was what he had been asking.

I attempted to find a common topic. Being a sports fan I thought of baseball. The Japanese love baseball. I swung my arms as if I had a bat in them and said, "Mr. Oh." Mr. Oh is the all time home run champion in Japan.

He swung his arms in the same manner and said, "Babe Ruth."

By this time many Scots were standing in a semi-circle around our table enjoying an American and a Japanese communicating with no common language. Many gyrations were being used, though.

As we were leaving I heard a rather meek voice calling "Meeky, Meeky." I turned around to see my new Japanese friend holding up my jacket that I had forgotten.

Mexico

While we were in Acapulco, Becky expressed a desire to "swim with the dolphins." A couple of days later we went to the natatorium.

She enjoyed the usual antics. The dolphin pushed her the length of the pool while she held her feet together. She held hoops the dolphin jumped through, and it leaped from the water to snatch something from her outstretched arm.

Since playing with the dolphins was high on her bucket list of things to do, we paid the extra dinero for private frolicking. Now she was paired with her own, private dolphin. He performed tricks, such as leaping completely over Becky from the bottom of the pool while she was standing erect.

On cue from the trainer the dolphin protruded half his body straight up out of the water to be hugged and kissed. The grand finale was that he would sing with Becky while she conducted the music like a maestro with an orchestra.

Again, the dolphin was half out of the water, facing my wife, who waved her arms as instructed and sang, "Row, row, row your boat." No response from her dolphin partner.

The trainer explained the problem. The dolphin did not know English. She should sing, "La Cucaracha." She did so, and you've never heard a more piercing attempt at singing for a couple of minutes. Go figure!

Germany

We had been at a home exchange for almost two weeks in Kiel, which is in the extreme northern part of the country. This was the home base for the German U-boats in World War II.

On numerous occasions we had driven by a particular liquor store. We enjoyed the German white wine so much we decided to send a case of our favorite home to America.

Three days before we were to depart we stopped at the liquor store at ten in the morning to make our purchase. Since the proprietor spoke no English, it took a while to let him know we wanted a case of white wine to ship. When he finally understood, he beckoned us to the rear of the store.

On a large barrel standing up were approximately twelve bottles of opened white wine. He insisted we taste them to decide which we preferred. He drank some of each along with us. Again, it was ten to ten-thirty. Needless to say, we were all in a mellow mood by the time we made our decision. He boxed it up and we headed for the post office.

We filled out the lengthy required postal document. Where it asked for contents, we wrote "wine." When we presented it all to the young postal clerk, he said in a loud voice, "Nein, nein, nein!" Though he spoke no English he made us understand it was illegal to send alcoholic beverages into the United States — a USA law.

"What shall we do?" we exclaimed.

He answered in very broken English, "Supervisor, supervisor," and pointed to a man at a desk.

Thankfully, the supervisor spoke English. We explained we were leaving Germany soon, and we couldn't possibly drink all the wine. What should we do?

He leaned forward and beckoned us closer. His solution: "Don't tell us what is in the package."

On our newly completed form we wrote "glassware" under contents. Package accepted. Wine mailed. Next please.

On a separate trip to Germany, this time to Munich, we decided to have a roadside picnic one lovely day. So off we went to a small German grocery. All signs were in German and no one spoke English. So, we shopped mainly by looking at the items.

Okay. Let's see. Bread. Cold cuts. Potato salad. Pickles. Small mayo and mustard. Beer and soda.

The night before, my wife had a high heel on her shoe break off, so we were in need of super glue, which we also placed on the grocery checkout belt.

The cashier went crazy! She must have believed we thought the glue was a foodstuff. She waved her arms saying "Nein" and shook her head negatively. She grasped her hands together and simulated trying to separate them to no avail, demonstrating how the glue cemented things together.

Finally, we convinced the store manager we understood, and she let us check out. It's scary to imagine, though, that had we not known what was in the tube and she had said nothing, it would have been a never-to-be-forgotten picnic lunch.

Ireland

Since my four grandparents immigrated to the USA, I am partial to the country of my roots. Or, as they say, "the old sod." On one of my journeys to Ireland, my wife and I went to the famous Cliffs of Moher. These steep bluffs overlook the ocean that periodically comes to an abrupt halt when waves crash into the stone precipice and sprays water magnificently.

There is a path leading up some four hundred feet to the crest of the cliffs. A look back reveals this water-crashing action along the entire range.

On the day we were there, it was rainy and misty. A bit windy. A bit cool. A typical, nasty, Irish day.

After we had walked the path about halfway up, I randomly asked a gentleman who was returning down the path with his wife, "Would you mind taking our picture?" He took my camera while we positioned ourselves against the wall providing the best background.

After taking a couple of shots, he handed my camera back and said, "You play golf at Diamondhead, don't you?"

I replied in shock, "Yes, I do."

"I have a picture of you on my fireplace mantle at home," he stated.

Unbelievable! Here on this rainy weekday in an out-of-the-way place, of all the people I could have sought to snap our picture, I chose him, a man from Slidell, Louisiana, with whom I had played in a pro-am golf tournament several years ago. What are the odds of that? It truly is a small but wonderful world.

The final occurrence I'll share with you is the closest to my heart. I had more knowledge about the background of my maternal grandfather than any of my grandparents. My mother and her sisters had told us of him and documented items regarding him.

Thomas Patrick McCormack's father brought Tom to the USA as a seventeen- year-old lad. His father's love motivated him to see that Tom had an opportunity to achieve a better life than available in Ireland. Of course, he would miss his only son profoundly. What an unselfish act of love.

So, on one of my trips to Ireland we made plans to research the family's past. We were aware that the McCormacks resided in the small town of Tulla, which is about a one-hour drive from the larger city of Limerick.

We began by going to the county courthouse, but their archives revealed little. Records were not maintained as they are today. A copy of the Census of 1901 listed Tom, his father, mother, and one sister. Also, his father was a proprietor of the small general store in Tulla. The county employees suggested the Catholic Church in Tulla, as the churches kept better records.

We ventured into Tulla seeking local information. Arriving at mid-morning on a Saturday, we proceeded to the local pub that had the most activity. After introducing ourselves, we explained our quest, seeking information about James McCormack (my great grandfather and Tom's father). No one remembered him but suggested that a gentleman in town, who is the town's historian, could possibly help us. The pub owner called this individual who showed up twenty minutes later. During the wait for him we provided fresh pints for everyone in appreciation of their efforts.

The town historian could not recall the McCormacks, but did state there was a commercial building on the main street that had the name McCormack etched in concrete over the entrance. This well may have been the location of his store. He too suggested we try the local church for information.

We located the church and rang the doorbell of the rectory. A pleasant, elderly priest answered. We again stated our desire for information. We explained that Tom was born in 1873. He seated us in a parlor and asked us to wait there.

When he returned some fifteen minutes or so later, he had an extremely large ledger book with him. There in black ink on one of the pages was the entry recorded attesting to the baptism of my grandfather. It read, "Tom P. McCormack, son of James and Mary Murnane McCormack baptized November 3, 1874." We took pictures of the entry.

Perhaps I am a sentimentalist, but evidence of the humanity of my forefather, whom I had never met, nearly brought me to tears. For so long I had admired the memory of his courage to follow his father's advice and leave his family forever. Now, here was an activity actually involving him. We had gone about as far as we could with our research.

The satisfaction of having some of our questions answered, of learning more about my ancestor, and finally witnessing the ledger recording an event as significant as his baptism brought him closer to me personally than I had ever dreamed.

It occurred to me that perhaps my love and enjoyment of travel goes back to the DNA or heredity of this grandfather, Tom McCormack.

Author's Note: TRAVEL TALES

My wife and I enjoy traveling. We find it interesting, educational, and enjoyable. The six countries in this presentation were selected because of the unusual events described. Many more could have been cited.

We never had a moment's problem with people everywhere returning kindness with kindness. The language and money exchange provided a challenge but never any major problem. We learned to seek out the young people (teenagers, etc.) for assistance. They are required to study multiple languages in school and most of the time one of them is English.

While some folks resist international travel, we highly recommend it. The memories we have are priceless. I hope you enjoyed us sharing a few.

Trees

Joyce Kilmer was right when he said, "I think that I shall never see a poem lovely as a tree."

Besides their aesthetic beauty, trees provide a useful service to mankind in all four seasons. In the spring, is there anything more encouraging as when the leaves return to their native homes, the trees? Everyone applauds the departure of winter and welcomes the arrival of milder weather. The trees join the flowers and other growth, bringing us pleasure.

Summer also embraces our trees. Now we have the luxury of the shade they provide. The birds and squirrels are pleased to see the return of their former perches. Children again can enjoy their tree houses. Some trees can be harvested and processed for timber to build our homes and work places.

No artwork equals the magnificence of trees in the fall. The variety of leaf colors blended as they are can be literally breathtaking. There is serenity in the atmosphere from the kaleidoscope of the tree's changing seasons.

Winter is, of course, the least of attractiveness of the trees. The leaves and growth of the trees have lost their color. The limbs are primarily barren. It is as if it brings an ending to the year. There is still utility from the trees. Logs heat our campfires. Our fireplaces burn, providing heat and light.

The biblical book of Genesis talks of the creation of man, followed by the addition of a woman. Supposedly they fell from the grace of God by eating a forbidden fruit, an apple. If this be the case, apple trees must have existed back to the Garden of Eden. That would make them one of earth's earliest creations. Should this be true, we give thanks to the Lord for giving us trees.

Taken for granted, it is a better world we live in with trees.

Author's Note: TREES

This piece was written to stimulate thought of a work of nature. We all live among various types of trees. Large and majestic, small and just beginning to grow, for appearance sake only, for useful utility.

They are just one of many of God's gifts we encounter daily and take for granted. Mother nature constantly affects our lives. I hope this small work will help you appreciate the many things that enhance your life.

Seeking a Lighthouse

"I'm really getting worried, John. The radio and TV stations say that the hurricane out in the Gulf is a huge one and could be headed our way. What do you think we should do?" Rebecca frowned.

"How many times have we been told that only to have the storm change course and move away from us? Let's face it; they really don't know for sure where it will land. Let's get all the plants and outdoor things inside and ride it out."

However, this time as Hurricane Katrina came ashore, Diamondhead, Mississippi, took the full strength of the storm.

That night, John and Rebecca lay huddled in their bed. They listened as the roar of the winds and torrential rain beating their house made eerie sounds.

"John, I'm scared," Rebecca sobbed.

"There's nothing we can do at this point," John said. "Let's just pray we'll survive."

At daybreak they ventured out. They had lost their power, telephone, and water. Scores of trees had been uprooted and fallen either to the ground or on their home. A big oak had damaged some of the brick structure. High winds damaged the roof, and shingles littered much of the ground.

Later in the morning Rebecca told John, "There are two water spots on the bathroom ceiling." She climbed into the attic and in a shaky voice yelled down, "The two rotating wind vents were blown away, and there are puddles up here. I'm afraid the ceiling might collapse."

"Well, thank God the rain has stopped, but we need to get that water out. Let's bail out as much as we can."

Rebecca scooped up water in a bucket and handed it down the steps to John, who dumped it in the yard. This laborious job took three grueling hours. By evening, they both were exhausted and had backaches.

The night after Katrina passed, they lay in the darkness, perspiring and holding each other. Then John made an announcement. "Rebecca, I didn't work hard a good part of my life to live like this. We will be moving."

The next morning John used his cell phone to call a friend in Metairie, Louisiana, a suburb of New Orleans fifty miles away. "Pete, this is John. Did the storm hit you? Only heavy rain, huh? We are uninhabitable with no utilities."

John listened.

"Well, come on over; you can stay with us."

"You're very kind, old friend. We'd welcome the opportunity to stay with you until things are somewhat normal. Let me get back to you. Thanks ever so much."

"Honey, the Wilsons invited us to stay with them. I told them we'd only stay as long as necessary."

"Thank God."

The next day John approached some construction workers who had come into Diamondhead. "If you will put a temporary cover over my roof, I'll pay you well."

They agreed.

"Let's pack both cars, but only with clothing and items we might use while we are away."

"I'm going to give our perishable good items to the Gonzales. They have a generator," said Rebecca.

Some selected valuables, like fur coats and silverware, were locked in two closets for more security. Then they instructed their few remaining neighbors, "Please keep an eye on the place while we're gone."

John turned to Rebecca. "Let's put a lamp in the front window. If it's ever illuminated, we'll know the electricity is functioning."

"They say it could be quite a while," Rebecca said.

On the drive to the Wilsons, the radio announced, "All Gulf states have been declared in a state of emergency. It is reported that Katrina was the most devastating hurricane in our country's history. Thousands of people are homeless and struggling for survival."

Each day at noon they made the drive over to their home, and for six weeks the disappointment every day was nerve-racking and stressful.

At last they drove to Diamondhead and John saw a beautiful sight. "Look! A light is on in the window!"

Rebecca began to cry.

"It won't be the most fun we've ever had, but let's get to work. We want to have our house in tip-top condition so we can put it on the market, sell it, and look for a new community to live in. This time we'll do our homework and find a home out of harm's way."

Rebecca nodded her head in agreement and smiled. "That's for sure!"

Author's Note: SEEKING A LIGHTHOUSE

We experienced the wrath of Hurricane Katrina. The damage truly was horrific. Large oak trees were blown over, uprooted, and fell on our house doing considerable damage. Our roof was partly blown away.

Having lost power, water, and telephone for six weeks, you can imagine the complete changes in our lives. As we lay in bed the second night after the storm, we determined we would change where we live soon. We did not want to experience a disaster of this magnitude ever again.

"Seeking a Lighthouse" describes our actions thereafter.

Experience of a PGA Tournament Director

Conducting a Professional Golf Association (PGA) tournament entails a variety of responsibilities: raising funds to provide the tournament its prize money; developing media relations; arranging for first aid capabilities; establishing a network of homes to provide housing for the players; recruiting and monitoring a large number of volunteers (e.g. 2,000) to keep score, manage the food outlets, and much more.

Despite all the preparations, one can usually expect the unexpected. Things occur that can't be foreseen or planned for.

The following two were experienced at one of the golf tournaments, The Nike Mississippi Gulf Coast Classic.

Greed

Many residents offer free lodging to the touring professional golfers who come into a town to participate in the local PGA tournament. This is a welcome arrangement to most of the golfers who seek to mini-mize their expenses.

We invited a young couple from California to use our guest bedroom. On Monday, at dinner in our home, Vic, the professional, mentioned he had hit practice balls at the golf course that day but the prac-tice balls were not those provided by the PGA for the practice range the week of the tournament. A week before each tournament, the PGA sends to the host golf club a large supply of new golf balls for the pros to use for practice.

Tuesday morning I visited the practice range. Sure enough, the balls available were used balls with cuts and bruises.

I then went to the pro shop of the club. Since the head golf professional wasn't there, I asked his assistants about the new range balls they had been sent. I was told, "They're in storage, and we've been instructed not to put them out." I insisted they summon the head golf pro to the shop.

When the club head pro arrived, he said, "I didn't put them out but intended to later in the week." I insisted that they be put out immediately. A shouting match ensued.

I reminded him the golf club and course was ours. "We paid handsomely to rent the facilities, and for one week it is our club."

After more heated exchanges, I took the boxes of balls to the practice range for the pros' use as they were intended. Upon completion of the tournament, I donated the golf balls to the local youth golf program, as the PGA suggests.

Several weeks later I received a telephone call. A man identified himself and stated, "I wanted to purchase some of the practice range golf balls used in the tournament." He said in previous years he purchased them from his barber who told him he didn't get any this year, but he could call me, and I could tell him where to get them.

I discovered that for the past several years, this club's head golf professional had not been providing many balls for the professionals to use, and not donating any to a youth golf program. Instead, he was selling them for personal profit. His club was not aware this was being done.

His lack of honesty in this and other matters caused him to be terminated by the golf club. At last report, he is no longer a golf professional and is presently employed at a Wal-Mart store.

Humor

On the final day of a tournament, the pairings order of play is determined by the standings of the remainder of the contestants. Those in last place tee off first. The final participants are the players with the two lowest scores. Following these players is always exciting because more often than not, one of these two will be the ultimate tournament winner. It is similar to dueling for the championship.

Besides the satisfaction of creating revenue for deserving charities, there are other perks that accompany tournament leadership. Becky and I arranged to be the two volunteers to walk with the last twosome so we could witness the competition up close.

Becky was the standard bearer and she carried a

cumbersome, long-poled scoreboard. I acted as the official scorekeeper and I carried an eight and one-half by eleven-inch clipboard to record each stroke both players executed. Scorekeepers and standard bearers, who accompany players, are trained by the PGA to walk several paces behind the participants so as not to distract them.

This particular day it was quite windy. On the third hole, as the players were walking down the fairway, Becky struggled to control her charge. I mused, "Boy, this clipboard sure is getting heavy." Not amused, she snapped with an irritated voice, "Why don't you put that clipboard where the sun doesn't shine!"

Both players stopped in their tracks and jerked around. First of all, we did not realize they heard us. Secondly, they did not know we knew each other. Finally, they had no idea we were husband and wife. They thought they were going to have to stop a fight. It was quite tense for a moment.

We explained we were married and were only joking. You could hear their sighs of relief. The balance of the day, we witnessed a very dramatic match between John Elliot and Skip Kendall that was not decided until the final hole.

We sometimes laugh at how, for a brief moment, we took center stage from the two combatants.

Author's Note: EXPERIENCES OF A PGA TOUR-NAMENT DIRECTOR

A book could be written of the various challenges that occur during the competition of a golf tournament. Every thing from: a player bitten by a bumble bee to, the performer, Vince Gill, showing up inquiring where he can park his bus, to providing bananas at the #1 and #10 tees for the players to intake potassium.

This story reveals but two of the incidents that happened at the same tournament conducted in Gulfport, Mississippi. Believe me, there could be more.

Experiences won an award in 2011 presented by the White County Creative Writers.

A New Beginning

"How's it going, Charles?"

"Divorce sucks!"

I chuckled. "Don't sugar coat it, man."

Charles and I had been buddies since grammar school some thirty years ago. We'd cried, laughed, played, and grown up together, but I 'd never seen him like this. His sunny disposition had gone south.

"Billy," he said, "I've second-guessed myself many times for divorcing Julia. We both know she's drop-dead gorgeous. She's no airhead, that's for sure. At the time we split, it just seemed our careers clashed and we had trouble getting on the same page. Now I wish we had worked it out."

I nodded and Charles continued. "I'll tell you this, coming home to an empty house after a hard day at work gets old. Sometimes I feel like I'm all alone on an isolated island."

I could identify with the problem. Until I married Alice three years ago, I was lonely too. Man isn't meant to be alone forever.

"What can I do about it? I'm a decent-looking guy with a good job. I enjoy having a good time and have no major vices. I'm in good health. You'd think that somewhere out there is someone who can connect with me. But where do I find her?"

"Have you tried a matchmaking service?"

"I signed with two different ones but have nothing to show for it."

"Charles, despite those past experiences, let me introduce you to a unique dating firm. I can tell you firsthand, they are more thorough, professional, and effective than the others. They cost more because they utilize proven, qualified people to handle your case, but they're worth it. Lifetime Together is how Alice and I became acquainted."

Charles frowned. "What makes them so different?"

"For openers, they have a 75 percent success rate. They've created and employ computer programs that help them analyze your makeup — your likes, dislikes, and individual characteristics. You'll have a series of personal interviews with trained psychologists and counselors who will input their observations and conclusions into your portfolio. Eventually, your profile will be downloaded and compared to hundreds of ladies seeking companionship. A committee of six will make the final selection to recommend to you. The last difference is you won't meet your potential mate early on. A blind date will be arranged for your first meeting so you can get to know one another in a pleasant, relaxed atmosphere. In fact, neither of you will be given a photo of the other. While they believe physical appearance is important, they have often found it detracts from the total person. It really is exciting!"

The next evening, I arrived home from work and Alice told me Charles had called her and asked many questions regarding Lifetime Together.

"What did you say?"

"I told him it was a time-consuming process. However, if he hung in there, he'd probably meet someone he'd enjoy who shared his interests. It was worth the effort." Alice laughed. "Then I said he could look at you and me as good examples."

A week later after the Tuesday bowling league, Charles and I were having a few beers, and he completely caught me off guard. "I decided to give Lifetime Together a shot," he said. "What the hell, I can afford the two hundred fifty dollars."

I saw little of Charles the next several weeks. He must have spent most of his spare time completing questionnaires and filling out biographical papers. When I briefly spoke with him on the phone, he commented, "I'm sure glad I didn't have to pay them by the page."

About three months later, after all the paperwork and six face-to-face interviews, Charles told me his profile was completed. He said they told him they'd identified a prime candidate to match with him. She was a local girl name Jay Jay. Their profiles were an extremely high match.

A reservation was made for a party of two in Charles' name at the Rendezvous', a romantic restaurant downtown. Charles was to arrive at 7:00 p.m. At 7:30, Roy, Charles' case manager, would accompany Jay Jay to the table to make the introductions, and then he would quietly depart.

The night of the dinner, Charles asked Alice to come to his place to pick out the perfect tie to go with his new suit. She said he was like a teenager preparing for his first prom.

Later, Charles told me he arrived at 7:00 on the dot. The wait until 7:30 was the longest thirty minutes of his life. A million thoughts ran through his mind:

Roy says Jay Jay's and my profiles reveal remarkable compatibility. In fact, they're one of the most similar he has ever seen. Boy, I sure hope he's right.

Don't forget, a loving companion is the goal; careers are secondary.

My buddy's thoughts were interrupted when he recognized Roy's voice behind him.

When he and Jay Jay met face-to-face, he said his mouth dropped open and Jay Jay gasped. He'd forgotten that Julia's family called her "Jay Jay," a nickname for Julia Joyce. They hadn't seen each other in three years. She was still lovely.

After the maître d' seated Julia, the two of them gazed at each other in silence. Charles was the first to speak. "I've thought of you so many times."

"You'll always be special to me," Julia replied.

Now Charles is back to his old self — grins every time I see him. Oh, by the way, he and Julia will retie the knot next month.

Author's Note: A NEW BEGINNING

I became interested in a story about a dating service while on vacation with my stepson and his wife. These two people had just about given up on ever marrying. They were in their thirties and not involved with anyone.

Helen's friends submitted her name while Steve figured, "I'll give it one more shot." So they did.

Now, five years later, they are still like honeymooners. You have never witnessed a more loving couple.

Thus I created a fictitious dating service. As you read, a strange series of events led the former husband and wife in the story back to each other unknowingly.

A happy ending is always enjoyable.

Rebirth

This was one of the worst chores I had to perform since Herbert's death. I hated going out in the cold, and I didn't enjoy filling the empty juice cartons with water. Besides, it was very difficult to lift the milk crates loaded with three water-filled cartons.

One of the advantages of living in Hot Springs, Arkansas, is that they have several fountains available where citizens can obtain clear, refreshing spring water free of charge. For years Herbert replenished the cartons and made the fountain run. He had been gone two years now, and the task was mine.

I parked in the only parking space open as I arrived at the fountain. The cars were parked so close together it was difficult to remove the three crates from my backseat.

Noting my dilemma, a tall distinguished-looking gentleman said, "Here let me help you." I stood next to him at the multi-fountain as we both began filling our respective containers.

He had large empty wine bottles to carry his water in. Quite expensive wine I noticed.

He nodded at me and smiled. "Hello, my name is Larry Nichols. What's yours?"

"I'm Veronica Walters. Thank you for

your assistance."

After we both had filled our vessels, Larry put my three crates back in the car for me. Having splashed water on our hands while using the faucets, both our hands were wet and, as a result, very cold.

Larry smiled again. "There is a little café down on the corner. What do you say we warm up with a cup of coffee?"

"Okay, I have some time. You mean the Arrow Café?"

"Yes."

"I'll meet you there."

An hour later I was surprised at how long Larry and I had chatted over several cups of coffee. He was so interesting and pleasant. I had not spent this long in conversation with anyone in quite a while. It was obvious we had much in common. He lost his wife, Susan, over four years ago. They had been married thirty-one years and he spoke fondly of her. It sounded like his life was somewhat empty like mine. Before we parted, he asked, "Would you mind if I called you sometime?"

"No, I'd like that." I gave him my telephone number.

I was a bit disappointed when I didn't hear from Larry right away. Three days later, I received a package in the mail. It was puzzling to me. When I opened it, there was a pair of gloves and a card stating, "You should always keep your hands warm." It was signed, "Fondly, Larry Nichols."

The following week I received a call from Larry and I was as excited as a teenager.

"My church is having a pot luck dinner next Tuesday. Would you like to go with me as my guest?"

"Are you sure it would be okay?"

"Of course, anyone can bring a guest, and there is no one I would rather be with."

"I'd be delighted. What should I bring?"

"Just yourself. I will take care of the rest. I'll pick you up at 5:30."

That evening I met many of Larry's friends. They were all gracious. I even got the feeling he had told some of them about me. They seemed eager to meet me. The thing that impressed me most was how well he was respected and liked by everyone. This reinforced my feeling that he was a decent man.

The following week I invited Larry to my home for dinner. It was exciting to be hosting a gentleman. It had been a long time. I spent hours preparing one of my best dishes, veal Marsala. I even lit candles on the table, which was an extreme rarity.

The dinner was wonderful. Besides the food, the table was graced with the flowers Larry had brought.

After dinner we moved to the living room and split a new bottle of pinot grigio. Once again the conversation was enjoyable.

As he was leaving, he said, "Thank you for the most delightful evening I have had in years." He hugged me and kissed me on the cheek as he left.

The first three meetings were so pleasant and such a joy that they were a catalyst for the beginning of a steady courtship. We saw each other two or three times a week from then on. Whether it be a movie, a dinner date, the theater or whatever, just being together increased our fondness for one another.

We learned a great deal about each other. For instance, he enjoyed reading, taking walks, would love to cruise but never had, had religious beliefs, and often listened to music.

He learned that I had a fear of flying, also was an avid reader, enjoyed the theater and dining.

Now, when we part, we kiss each other. Not courtesy kisses but affectionate ones.

Several months later my birthday was on a Friday. Larry wanted to do something special for me. He made dinner reservations at the most romantic restaurant in the metropolitan area, The Back Porch. Situated on Lake Hamilton, it featured a spectacular sunset view.

Larry said he had a special dessert planned for us. After dinner we drank our coffee as two waiters approached our table. Each had a glass plate encased by a silver cover.

Simultaneously, they laid each plate in front of us and removed the covers in unison.

In the middle of my plate was a jewelry box. When I opened the box, it revealed a beautiful diamond ring. I gasped.

"Veronica, will you marry me?"

I had to pause to catch my breath. "I had hoped you'd propose some time. Of course, I will."

The entire restaurant applauded as we leaned across the table and kissed each other.

While Herbert will always be my first love and Susan will always be Larry's first love, our union has brought joy and meaning to our lives. We truly love each other.

By the way, for our honeymoon I agreed to fly to New Orleans. From there we are taking a seven-day cruise to the Caribbean.

Nowadays when we restock our water supply, we go together. It is no longer a dreaded chore. It is a reminder of our relationship. You might call it the fountain of rebirth.

Author's Note: REBIRTH

This story was inspired by an observation. One day while I was refilling our bottles with fresh, clear, spring water in Hot Springs.

An elderly lady drove up to do likewise. She appeared rather frustrated. A distinguished-looking gentleman offered to assist her removing her vessels from her auto.

They stood next to each other and talked while performing their task. "Rebirth" is an accounting of the progression of Larry and Veronica. The story illustrates that you're never too old to enjoy life.

THE END

About the Author

Mickey Jordan is a graduate of the University of Tennessee – Knoxville. He had a very successful business career culminating in owning and operating his own financial services firm. During his business life he authored numerous articles that were published in local, state, and national journals. Upon retirement he turned his efforts to writing short stories. Many of his stories, including some in "Kaleidoscope of Tales," have won awards in literary competitions.

Mickey resides in Hot Springs Village, Arkansas, with his wife, Becky. They have six children and ten grandchildren. He is a member of the Hot Springs Village Writers' Club. He also is an active participant of the Village Writers' Critique Group.

www.ingramcontent.com/pod-product-compliance
Lightning Source LLC
Chambersburg PA
CBHW051253170626
46809CB00004B/1620